"You're upset with me."

Sheri saw the raw vulnerability in Mark's taut features as he spoke. She opted for honesty. "I'm a little wary of the effect we have on each other. I know we agreed there would be no kissing, but I'm not too sure I'd be able to hold you to your promise."

"Why? What's wrong with giving in to what we both want?"

When her gaze shifted to the partially open door and the long, dimly lit hallway beyond, understanding warmed his eyes. "If we got carried away, all I'd have to do is sweep you up in my arms and head down that hall until I found the bedroom."

She didn't answer as his thumb glided across her lower lip, his touch light and deft, sensitizing her mouth until it quivered. "Wh—what about our agreement?" she gasped.

"I'm not kissing you." The color of his eyes deepened to smoky blue. "I just want to see if you're as hungry as I am." He brought his mouth to within an inch of hers. "Next time, no agreements."

Dawn Carroll is a new but extremely popular author for us. Her first Temptation romance, *Code Name Casanova*, is still garnering rave reviews and fans! A native of California, Dawn is busy with her family and writing. She is a bit of a perfectionist, though—while researching auto thefts, her *own* car was stolen and she received her first traffic citation in fifteen years! Dawn is threatening to write a book about a heroine who wins the lottery—to see if it will happen to her too!

Books by Dawn Carroll

HARLEQUIN TEMPTATION
268–CODE NAME CASANOVA

Naughty Thoughts
DAWN CARROLL

Harlequin Books

TORONTO • NEW YORK • LONDON
AMSTERDAM • PARIS • SYDNEY • HAMBURG
STOCKHOLM • ATHENS • TOKYO • MILAN

For Jean,
a friend in all seasons.
And for Marce, Teresa and Virginia,
fellow dream weavers all.
With a very special thank-you to Sergeant Ed Becker,
Auto Theft Strike Unit, San Diego Police Department.

Published July 1991

ISBN 0-373-25454-7

NAUGHTY THOUGHTS

Printed in U.S.A.

1

"A BELLY DANCER?" Police Sergeant Mark Sampson rolled his eyes in disgust and slouched into his chair. "It's bad enough you coerced me into coming here tonight." He indicated the smoky back room of Kelly's Tavern with a wave of his hand. "Now I'm expected to watch some sleazy broad strut her stuff? Give me a break, Lou."

Mark's fellow officer Lou Reyes grinned, his teeth a bright slash in the Hispanic darkness of his face. He grabbed one of the frosty mugs of beer from their table, which was right on the edge of the tiny dance floor. After taking a quick swig, he advised, "Take it easy, pal. This lady's a class act. And you have to admit we needed something special to celebrate old Joe Hobbs tying the knot after all these years." He toasted his friend. "Besides, what did you expect at a bachelor party—blue movies?"

Mark scanned the casually dressed group of off-duty detectives crowding the room. Scattered throughout the predominantly male gathering were a few women officers, hardy souls who obviously considered their presence a score for women's equality. "I'm sure the ladies would love an X-rated show," Mark said, feeling his mouth quirk into a reluctant smile. "But I hate to think what the good citizens of San Diego would have to say if they found out."

Lou chuckled. "Precisely why I arranged for Sheri to entertain us. Even the *good* citizens won't be able to object to her." He narrowed his eyes consideringly and studied Mark's face. "You know, you should smile more often. My sister Tina says the female portion of the word processing department nearly swooned the last time you smiled at them. They voted you hunk of the month."

"Knock it off, Lou." Mark hunched his shoulders and hastily took a deep swallow of beer. He could feel his neck growing uncomfortably warm under the collar of his shirt and hoped his tan was dark enough to cover the telltale color.

"Hey, if your best buddy can't tell you, who can?" Lou rocked back in his chair, obviously enjoying himself. "Unfortunately for me, the ladies seem to prefer blue eyes and sun-bleached hair. You could have your pick of the flock if you'd loosen up a little. Hell, you could have the whole flock."

"Unlike some people I could name, I don't feel compelled to date every unattached female in the city. . . . No, make that county. I have better things to do with my time."

"Like fertilizing the rutabagas in that overgrown garden of yours?" Lou snorted.

"I don't grow rutabagas, but even if I did, I'd at least have something to show for my time afterward."

Lou's grin was unabashed. "I've got memories, pal. And you might have a few, too, after tonight's entertainment. Speaking of which, I see she's arrived. I'll be right back." He stood up and started toward the rear door.

A woman stood just inside, her body swathed from head to toe in yards of shimmering white material. The veil covering her face revealed only a pair of dark eyes—the artfully painted eyes of a seductress.

Mark scowled. He had a few memories of his own when it came to women and a particular aversion to *her* kind. Arms folded across his chest, he sat back in his chair, prepared to endure.

Lou clapped his hands for attention and announced in grandiose tones, "Ladies, gentlemen, let's give a warm welcome to our entertainer, Scheherazade, Jewel of the Desert."

Mark uttered a sigh and stared at the ceiling. But a moment later, curling strains of Middle Eastern music drew his attention to the dance floor directly in front of him. Scheherazade stood in the center of a small spotlight, and as the music swelled, she began to move, the white material flowing around her in silky ripples. Like a slender flower caught in a warm summer breeze, she followed the music, her movements a part of the lilting symphony.

Fascinated in spite of himself, Mark leaned slightly forward.

The tempo quickened and the sheer folds shifted apart, allowing a brief, tantalizing view of pale, satin-soft skin. Her graceful arms drifted up, and tiny cymbals flashed at the ends of her fingers with a sharp ching. Then, with mesmerizing slowness, she began to unwind the concealing drapery. An appreciative murmur rose from the audience as Scheherazade teasingly revealed more and more of her undulating body.

Mark shifted uncomfortably and tried to hold on to his objectivity. Okay, so the act wasn't as tawdry as he'd expected—so far. That didn't excuse the concept. Did she get her kicks out of turning on a roomful of men?

Probably. *Just look at that outfit.* The top was nothing more than a bra—a skimpy one—with several layers of silvery fringe to draw attention to the lush curve of her breasts. And the flimsy skirt revealed more of her long shapely legs than it concealed. How she managed to keep it on was beyond him. The intricately beaded and fringed waistband rode dangerously low on her perfectly rounded hips— beautiful hips that moved in silent, provocative invitation. Luring him . . . promising ecstasy . . . making him wonder how it would feel. . . .

"She's got the kind of body sultans must dream about," Lou muttered, his gaze fixed on Scheherazade's gently fluttering belly.

Mark shook his head dazedly. What was happening here? His body felt taut as a bowstring, and low in his gut there was an unmistakable stirring, a blossoming heat.

He jerked upright and reached for his beer just as the dance ended and applause broke out. The cold bite of the brew felt good on his dry throat and he drank deeply, hoping the chill would reach his stomach—and lower. Damn it! The whole idea was ridiculous. She was the very antithesis of everything he wanted in a woman. How could she possibly have any effect on him?

"See what you've been missing, old pal?" Lou laughed and leaned closer to confide, "If you're real nice to me I might introduce you to her. She and my sister are friends. Tina's been taking Sheri's belly-dancing class for a couple years."

"Thanks, but no thanks," Mark replied, sitting back once again with arms crossed. A belly-dancing teacher. What kind of living could she make doing that? Probably supplemented it with a little topless dancing in some bar, or, worse yet—

A silvery clash of tiny cymbals signaled the beginning of Scheherazade's next dance, and Mark's eyes were drawn to the source of the sound. *Scratch hooker*, he told himself, scrutinizing her face for the first time. He'd been a beat cop long enough to know the look of a pro when he saw one, and in spite of his prejudices against dancers, he had to admit she didn't qualify. The eyes might be heavily made-up, but there was a guileless charm in the way she flirted with them, as if she'd never had to evaluate her allure in monetary terms. And the smile lacked the calculated sensuality of a street girl's. In fact she had a lovely mouth, the lips soft and just full enough to make a man think about kissing them.

He narrowed his eyes, imagining the feel of her mouth beneath his. Soft . . . yes, and eager. Lips parting . . .

He found himself leaning forward, his arms resting on the table. *I'd like to kiss you until there wasn't a bit of that garish red lipstick left, little dancer.*

As if she'd heard, Scheherazade met his gaze and moved a little closer to his table. A strange excitement surged through Mark, unlike anything he'd felt in a long time. He discovered he couldn't look away, some compulsion deep inside him wouldn't allow it. She radiated sensuality like a hot summer sun, warming parts of him he'd thought frozen and dead.

Her skin gleamed like alabaster as she executed a graceful turn, the hem of her skirt flaring. She was closer now, so close the swish of her veil brought a whiff of her exotic scent, a bewitching combination of flowers and musk and warm feminine skin. Mark inhaled deeply, savoring her essence.

Her long hair swirled over her shoulders, the dark brown waves glinting with red highlights. How would it feel to sink his fingers into that silky hair? To feel her warm, vibrant body beneath his, her breasts gently crushed against his chest, her softly curved belly moving in exciting counterpoint to his every thrust?

The music ended in a ringing crescendo, and Mark came out of his daydream to the embarrassing reality of a raging erection pushing against the fly of his conservative tan slacks. Fortunately the table hid his condition from view, but he found little comfort in that. Especially when Lou offered to bring the dancer over for introductions.

"Forget it!" Mark replied a little too sharply. If she came over here, he'd have to stand up and the whole damn room would see. "No offense," he added placatingly. "But I'm not interested. In fact, I'm going to leave as soon as I finish my beer." Too bad he couldn't dump the stuff onto his crotch—it'd probably do more good there.

"Suit yourself," Lou retorted. With one hand he gave a self-conscious sweep to his thick black hair. "I'm going to thank her for coming tonight. Who knows? I might get lucky."

As he watched his friend join the small crowd gathering around the dancer, Mark felt an odd flash of anger. Not that he wanted the woman for himself. Hot daydreams aside, she still wasn't his type. But it grated a little to think of her ending up in another man's arms so soon after being the object of his own fantasy.

Man, that really sounded rational, an inner voice mocked. Mark shook his head and shoved aside his unfinished drink. The whole evening had been irrational, particularly his unexplainable response to the sultry-eyed temptress. Maybe Lou was right. Maybe he should date more often. The problem with that was, he felt guilty enough about the nights he was called to the field and had to leave April with a sitter.

Thinking of his perky eight-year-old daughter softened his grim expression to tenderness; it also cooled the last of his ardor. With a sigh of relief he rose and headed for the door, about ten paces behind the exiting dancer.

SCHEHERAZADE, more commonly known as Sheri O'Reilly, stepped out into the trash-littered alley behind Kelly's Tavern and expelled a deep sigh. The crisp dampness of the night air felt good after the stuffy warmth of Kelly's back room, even if it did raise a few goose bumps on her arms. If she was lucky, the chill might shock some sense back into her head, or at least dislodge the sensual images lingering there. Images of a lean-featured stranger with the hottest blue eyes she'd ever encountered.

She'd noticed him right away, slouching back in his chair, disapproval of her evident in every line of his face as she began to dance. Irritated, she had resolved to ignore him, but something had kept drawing her eyes back to his angular features.

As grouches went, he wasn't bad looking, handsome, if you liked the lean, tough type. His hair was unusual, too, pale ash woven thickly into a darker blond with a deep widow's peak that emphasized a strong forehead. Probably a precursor of baldness, she'd added uncharitably when she caught him scowling at her again.

The next time she'd glanced at him, however, a subtle change had taken place on the austere face. The deep grooves bracketing his mouth had softened somehow, as had the frown lines on his forehead. His blue eyes, so frigid moments before, radiated a surprising heat. She could have sworn she actually felt that warmth the moment he focused on her lips. And an instant later a terse challenge invaded her thoughts.

I'd like to kiss you until there wasn't a bit of that garish red lipstick left, little dancer.

The words couldn't have been clearer if he'd spoken them aloud, and they exerted a magnetic force, willing her to move closer to him. Almost without realizing she did so, she'd danced nearer and been rewarded by a narrowing of those smoky-blue eyes and the slightest flaring of his nostrils.

And then the truly shocking part had come. A startling image had begun to form in her mind, and with each seductive movement of her body it had become clearer, brighter. A vivid impression of the two of them lying together. Naked. She'd almost been able to feel his hard body pressing down upon hers with feverish need, almost taste the scorching hunger of his mouth. Their bodies had arched together, emulating the motions of her dance.

Or had it been the other way around? It had been difficult to tell while staring into the burning blue of his eyes. In fact, it had been hard to focus on anything aside from the sensual tension building within her body. Then the dance had ended abruptly, bringing the vision to an end as well, and she'd nearly collapsed at the letdown.

The sound of a car door slamming jolted Sheri out of her distracted thoughts. Realizing she had been standing there on the dank pavement of Kelly's back lot, reliving the whole bizarre incident, she shook her head and dug around in her capacious tote for her car keys. "Imagination, that's all it was," she muttered to herself. "Maybe Tina's right about my needing to date more often."

Keys in hand at last, she got a grip on the folds of the veil swathing her body and started toward her car, one of a dozen lining the cramped parking area. But she froze when an engine roared to life and her classy little Mercedes 450SL lurched out of its slot and headed straight for her. Shock, then searing outrage obliterated any thought of self-preservation. Hands on hips she stood her ground and hollered, "Hey, that's my car!"

The interior of the approaching automobile was dark, but she got a fleeting impression of a beefy face set in grim determination. Too late she realized the driver had no intention of stopping and she tensed in anticipation of a painful impact. Instead she felt something hard wrap around her waist, hauling her back and around until she bumped into a solid surface. In the next instant, an equally solid body crushed against her. A heavy rush of air buffeted her as the car roared by, then the body shielding hers eased back a little, allowing her a glimpse of her car's brake lights as it careened out of the alley and disappeared.

"Are you all right?" a husky male voice inquired.

"I . . . I think so," she gasped, her breathing labored. A moment later, however, she remembered the cause of their near miss and her outrage returned. "My car! That creep just stole my car!" She pushed against the substantial male chest that still sandwiched her to Kelly's dingy back wall. The chest obligingly moved back, and she looked up into a pair of impossibly blue eyes.

They narrowed censoriously as their owner spoke again. "He also tried to run you down. Don't you have any sense of self-preservation, lady? You could have been killed."

Sheri tried to shrug off his judgmental stare, but stopped when she realized his pelvis was still jammed hard against hers and his forearms remained propped on the wall, bracketing her head. She felt an uncustomary flush bloom on her cheeks. "Uh, if you don't mind..." She exerted a little more pressure against his chest, and taut muscles flexed beneath her fingers as he pushed away from the wall and took a step back.

Unfortunately, her body chose that moment to react to the reality of her near brush with death. Her knees buckled and she would have slid to the ground if her rescuer hadn't caught her. He scooped her into his arms and started toward the back door of Kelly's.

"You'd better go inside and sit down for a while. You've had a bad scare," he said with unexpected gentleness.

A grand reentry in this man's arms? That was the last thing she wanted. Especially when she glanced down and discovered her veil had been twisted until it no longer covered her, and her skirt had somehow been torn from the hem right up to the beaded belt. She could imagine what it would look like if they rejoined the party inside. She began to struggle. "No, wait. I have to do something about my car. You can put me down. I'm fine, really."

"Quit squirming around like that, or I'm liable to drop you," he responded tersely, staggering a little as her efforts to escape became more forceful.

They both stopped cold when a third voice commented dryly, "Jeez, Mark, are the strong-arm tactics really necessary? I offered to introduce you to the lady." Lou stood just outside the back door of Kelly's, a wide grin on his face.

"This isn't what it looks like . . ." Mark began, but Sheri overrode him.

"Lou, thank heaven you're here. You've got to do something." She renewed her efforts to wriggle free of the surprisingly strong arms that held her. Appearances and propriety were no longer her only motives. Her main concern was her car. A sick emptiness yawned inside her as the reality of her loss hit home. She wanted to scream in denial, to have it all turn out to be a bad dream.

Lou leaned back against the building. "Looks to me like Mark has the situation well in hand. Although I guess I should introduce you. Sheri, meet my best buddy, Mark Sampson. Mark, your charming armful is Sheri O'Reilly. And I think you'd better put her down before she decides to hit you."

"This is no time for social pleasantries!" Sheri cried as Mark allowed her feet to slide to the ground. She stepped away from him quickly, gratified that her legs seemed to be working again. "Some jerk just stole my car and nearly ran me over in the process."

Lou's grin faded. "No kidding? Hey, I'm sorry, I thought—"

"Never mind what you thought," Sheri interrupted, trying in vain to hitch up the slipping folds of her veil. "What are you going to do about it? I happen to know you're in charge of the auto-theft department in this city."

"Half of the auto-theft department," Lou corrected. "And not the half you need. My division is reactive. I deal with cases where the guy's already in custody." He smiled ruefully. "Your luck isn't all bad, though. You landed in the arms of the man who can help you." He indicated his friend with a lift of his chin. "Sergeant Sampson is in charge of the proactive division."

Sheri turned to the other man in time to see a flash of annoyance cross his taut features. "Damn it, Lou, you know we don't handle individual cases like this. I don't have the time or the manpower to chase every kid who decides to do a little joyriding. What she needs is a beat cop to take her report."

"Joyriding?" Sheri knew her eyes had widened. "How can you dismiss it like that? The guy tried to run me down!"

"Only because you refused to get out of his way," Mark countered, his own irritation plain to see.

Sheri felt her temper begin to slip again. He made it sound as if the whole thing were her fault. "I was trying to stop that crook from stealing my car. There didn't seem to be any police around who were willing to do the job."

The flash of anger in Mark's eyes indicated he hadn't missed her implication. "I was a little busy trying to save your life," he said through gritted teeth. "*That* is a peace officer's first priority."

"Hey, kids, no fighting," Lou interjected, his hands held up placatingly. "Mark, couldn't you at least take the crime report info from her? It'd save calling out a patrol car. And you *were* involved in the incident."

When Mark grudgingly agreed, Lou turned to Sheri. "I think you should go back inside first. It's chilly out here, and you're starting to turn a little blue."

Until then, Sheri hadn't noticed she was shivering, but she shook her head vehemently. "Not looking like this." She indicated her torn skirt. "I don't care to be the object of lurid conjecture." She knew only too well how that felt.

Mark gave a short bark of laughter. "Then you sure picked the wrong profession. A while ago you had every man in that room lusting after you."

The censure in his voice hit her like a swift punch. Once again she'd been tried and convicted by appearances alone. Combined with the other emotions roiling inside her, his criticism was too much to bear. She lashed back without considering the possible consequences. "Including you, Sergeant Sampson? I saw the way you looked at me. Is that why you don't think I deserve your esteemed help in finding my car? Does my dancing somehow make me a second-class citizen?"

Lou regarded Mark with dawning perception. "How did you look at her? Did I miss something here?"

Mark bit back a curse and wondered how in the world things had deteriorated to this point. Lou looked like a man who had caught his best friend *in flagrante delicto*, and the woman—for heaven's sake—looked as if she were fighting tears.

Okay, maybe he shouldn't have made that last crack, but damn it, all she'd done was vituperate since he'd pulled her from the path of the speeding car. His pulse still hadn't calmed completely from the close call they'd had. That and the undeniable thrill of holding her lush body in his arms, he amended honestly. A thrill like nothing he felt with the "acceptable" women he occasionally saw. And therein lay the source of his antagonism toward her.

What was needed here was a quick exit, he told himself. But first he had to deal with the matter of her stolen car. "Look," he said, coming to a swift decision. "If it'll make you feel better, we can sit in my car while I get the necessary details for the crime report."

"Good idea," Lou put in, cutting off Sheri's quick refusal. "And while you're at it, could you possibly give her a lift home? I'm the designated driver tonight and I've got a carful."

"I don't need a ride from him," Sheri denied hotly. "I'd rather take a cab."

For some reason that irritated Mark even more. "Dressed as you are?" he inquired sarcastically. "You might end up with more than a stolen car to report. Even cabdrivers are human." Damn, did he just agree to give her a ride home?

"He's got a point, Sheri," Lou added for good measure.

"But . . ."

"No buts. You're my sister's friend, and I'm not going to let you take any unnecessary risks."

From the look on her face, it was clear Sheri considered riding with Mark an unnecessary risk, but she surprised him by agreeing at last.

As she followed Mark toward a tan and navy Bronco, Sheri decided he had to be the most disagreeable man she'd ever met. All those images she'd experienced earlier had to have been her imagination. This man didn't have an ounce of warmth or passion anywhere in his body. He probably hated kids and animals too, she tacked on sullenly.

She was forced to reevaluate her last assumption when he opened the Bronco's passenger door and a colorful cascade of boxes tumbled to the ground. "Girl Scout cookies?" she inquired. A soft laugh escaped her when she saw the back of the vehicle was packed to capacity with cartons bearing the familiar logo. "Either you mugged an entire troop, or your wife's a troop leader."

"My wife is dead," Mark said shortly. He shoved the fallen boxes back inside and tried to make room for her on the seat. "But even if she weren't, she wouldn't have involved herself with anything as maternal as Girl Scouts. I'm the one who gets sweet-talked into helping the cookie chairperson." He glanced back at her and as their gazes caught and held, an odd sensation—like the ache of an old wound—bloomed in the region of her heart. It lasted until he turned away, grabbed the jacket lying on the driver's seat and tossed it to her.

"Here, put this on. You look like you're going to shiver into a million pieces."

Sheri caught the jacket, but was too taken aback to put it on right away. Something strange had occurred between them during that brief look—something her mind tried to deny, even as her soul acknowledged it. A bittersweet memory washed over her, a dim recall of the silent communication she and her twin brother Sean had shared when they were children.

Only this time the hurt she'd felt hadn't been Sean's. It had come from the stoic-featured man standing before her. Knowing that led to an even more distressing thought. Maybe it hadn't been her overactive imagination painting all those erotic pictures in her mind as she danced. Cognition sent a shiver down her spine as she remembered the hot sensual images and her body's response to them.

"Are you going to get in or stand out here and freeze?" Sergeant Sampson's impatient inquiry made her realize he had managed to clear a place for her on the seat and was waiting for her to take it.

Frowning, Sheri climbed up and into the seat, pointedly refusing his offered hand. Now was not the time to be reliving that outrageous dance episode. But when she slipped her arms into the jacket, which looked like something a *Top Gun* pilot would wear, the elemental scent of leather, citrusy after-shave and man brought another wave of remembrance. As she had danced, the masculine hunger in his eyes had warmed her, even as his jacket warmed her now....

She pulled herself up sharply. What in the world was going on with her? She barely knew the man, and what she did know she didn't like. Yet the sensual pull between them was stronger than anything she'd felt in years.

"You look angry enough to bite my head off. Would it help if I apologized for what I said about your dancing?"

Startled by his bid for conciliation, she said stiffly, "I don't need an apology, I just want to go home. What information do you need for your report?"

He shook his head. "If you don't mind, I'd like to get us out of here before we do that. This isn't exactly the best neighborhood at night—as I'm sure you now know."

Unwilling to admit he was right, Sheri pulled the oversize jacket tighter around her and gave him directions to her house. As they proceeded out of the seedy area of lower Broadway, she stared out the side window, brooding.

The thought of some lowlife driving around in her beloved Mercedes made her feel as if she'd been violated. And as if that weren't enough, there was her bizarre reaction to the man sitting next to her. What an evening!

"Was that growl directed at me?"

The quietly voiced question made her look at him in surprise. "No. I was thinking about the guy who has my car."

"He'll probably ride around for a while and then abandon it. That's how the majority of auto thefts turn out. But even if he doesn't, you can always get another with the insurance payoff. You *do* have insurance, don't you?"

"Of course I have insurance," she snapped. "What kind of irresponsible idiot do you think I am?"

He hesitated and sent a telling look over her flimsy harem costume, his attitude clearly judgmental. It infuriated Sheri.

"You think you have me pegged, don't you, Sergeant Sampson?" She slurred the pronunciation of his title as though it were a swear word. "You think I'm some stupid little bimbo who hasn't got the sense to prevent her car from being stolen."

"Now just a minute, I didn't—"

"You probably think it's no more than I deserve, considering the life I must lead. Right? Well, let me set you straight on a few facts, *Sergeant*. Number one, belly dancing isn't my vocation, it's something I do because I enjoy it. But even if I did earn my living that way, it still wouldn't give you the right to judge me. I pay my taxes, I don't break the law and I don't look down on others just because their life-styles don't happen to conform to my standards."

She turned her back to him and pretended an intense interest in the colorful assortment of street people parading the sidewalks of upper Broadway. Another eloquent sigh came from the driver's side of the car, but Sheri continued to stare out the window as they headed away from the towering skyscrapers of downtown toward the hilly suburbs embracing the landward side of the city. To the west, San Diego Bay glinted coldly in the cloud-shadowed moonlight.

The silence between them had reached an unbearable level by the time the Bronco pulled up in front of her modest frame house. Sheri had the door open and was halfway out almost before the vehicle stopped. Turning, she said, "Thanks a lot for the ride, *Sergeant*." Then, with every ounce of her strength, she slammed the door.

She raced up the walkway and unlocked her front door with trembling fingers. But just before she got it closed behind her, a strong male hand wrapped itself around the edge and pushed it open again.

As she stared in disbelief, Mark Sampson stepped inside and announced firmly, "All right, you've had your say. Now it's my turn."

2

WITH NEARLY SIX FEET of determined male looming over her, Sheri did what any sensible woman would do—she backed up. After two steps, however, she bumped into the wall of the narrow hallway. "Sergeant Sampson, you can't . . ." she began uneasily.

"Would you stop acting like I'm about to jump you? And cut out the Sergeant stuff. My name is Mark, and I think this whole mess can be straightened out a lot faster if we switch to first names." He turned to close the door and lock it, then faced her. "Now, do you want to talk standing up, or are you going to offer me a seat?"

Sheri made a determined grab for her composure and waved him into the living room with an exaggerated flourish, then reached to switch on the lights. The movement caused the jacket she still wore—his jacket—to slip off one shoulder. "I suppose you came in to get this," she said, shrugging out of the supple garment as she followed him. She waited until he'd seated himself in a golden plush wing chair before tossing the garment to him.

"No, I'm here to take your statement on the car theft...." He hesitated, looked down and fiddled with the zipper on his jacket. "And to apologize. I've never considered myself a prejudiced man." He glanced up, smiled self-consciously and added, "Hard as that may be for you to believe. I'm really sorry I upset you, especially after the traumatic evening you've had. In fact, I think you'd better sit down. You still look a little shaky."

Sheri felt shaky, all right, but it wasn't entirely due to her earlier adventures. It was the grin, she decided, her anger dissipating like mist on a warm summer morning. The splendor of his smile transformed him. Twin grooves bracketed his mouth, framing a flash of perfect white teeth, and smile lines appeared at the outer corners of his eyes, drawing attention to their brilliant color.

When those eyes flickered downward, sweeping over her body in an utterly masculine appraisal, she was abruptly reminded how much naked skin her harem dancer's costume revealed. What had happened to the veil she used as a wrap? She must have dropped it somewhere in all the excitement.

"I...I'd like to change before we start." Good grief, even her voice was shaky. "I also could use a cup of coffee," she added, trying for a more normal tone. "Would you like some?"

He jerked his gaze back up to her face, then looked away. "Uh, coffee would be great."

Sheri didn't linger. With a muttered, "Make yourself comfortable," she turned and fled to the relative safety of her kitchen.

Watching her hasty retreat, Mark let out an exasperated breath. What was it with this woman? One minute he could barely contain his disapproval of her. The next he was ogling her body, wondering what she'd do if he pushed her down onto the couch and kissed her until she was breathless.

Speaking of the couch... His eyes narrowed, really taking in the room's decor for the first time. Compared to the quiet beiges and browns of his own conservative living room, this place looked positively sybaritic. The walls were a rich plum red, a color repeated in the gold-threaded floral brocade adorning the couch and windows. Tables and chairs stood on slender curving legs of gleaming dark wood, and a large gilt-framed mirror hung on one wall. Elegantly framed prints, which on closer scrutiny proved to be antique circus bills, graced the other walls, and an elaborate Turkish rug covered a large portion of the polished wooden floor. The overall effect was far too voluptuous for his taste, Mark decided.

And then there was the horse.

Suspended on a brass pole in one corner pranced a gleaming white carousel pony, his golden mane and tail flaring, his ornate saddle streaming colorful ribbons. The exotic beauty of the graceful creature blended perfectly with the ambience of the room.

Mark inhaled slowly. The place even smelled seductive, but not in the way he would have expected. In addition to the rich, dark aroma of brewing coffee, the air had a faint sweetness, as if someone had been baking earlier in the day. Baking? That didn't fit his image of a woman who spent her evenings dancing half-naked. . . .

He cut the thought off and shifted restlessly in his chair. He'd had enough of that kind of thinking for one night. Jaw set, he fixed his gaze on the sprightly horse and tried to calm his stirring libido.

When Sheri returned a short while later, Mark told himself she no longer resembled the enchantress who'd driven an entire room of men to lust, but his body still wasn't convinced. Even with her face free of makeup and her long hair pulled back in a clip, she still radiated a basic sensuality that made his pulse quicken. The striking purity of her features reminded him of his favorite, old-time movie stars, the kind of women who looked outstanding even on black-and-white film. And beneath the flowing peacock-blue gown she wore, there was a figure to match.

"How do you like your coffee?" Hands propped on her hips, Sheri eyed him warily, making him realize he'd been staring again.

"Black," he said, his response sharpened by chagrin. He added a softer "Please," when she frowned.

Nodding, she left the room again and returned a few minutes later with two steaming mugs. When he took a quick sip, Mark got yet another surprise. Mixed with the potent richness of coffee were the distinct flavors of chocolate and almond.

"Sorry," she murmured, noting his reaction. "I forgot to tell you it was flavored."

"No problem. It's quite good, actually." Down-right seductive, he added to himself. Just like every-thing else about her. He needed to get his mind back on the job at hand. He fished a small pad and pencil out of his jacket pocket and assumed a businesslike tone. "First I'll need your full name."

"Scheherazade," she began, then bristled at the look he sent her way.

"I mean your real name," he elaborated, secretly relieved to feel the return of their earlier antagonism. This way, at least, he didn't have to worry about get-ting the hots for her again. Right now she looked as approachable as an outraged porcupine.

"That *is* my real name," she said through gritted teeth. "My mother thought it would look great on a marquee."

"Your mother's in the theater?" Now that did fit.

"No, she was in a circus."

Mark's gaze flickered to the pony, then the posters.

"You can just wipe that look off your face, Ser-geant Sampson. I don't really care what you think of me or my background."

"It's Mark," he corrected automatically. But he knew there was no hope of civility between them, even if she had misread his expression. They were just too different. By the time he'd finished noting the in-formation he needed, the tension between them had become almost palpable. They walked to her front door in stony silence, but she spoke first when he turned to say good-night.

"How long will it take you to find my car?"

Suppressing a groan, Mark attempted diplomacy. "I'm afraid you've gotten the wrong impression. We can't investigate every stolen vehicle report that comes in. My division has neither the manpower nor the time. As I told you before, your car could turn up in a few days, most likely deserted by the roadside because the thief tired of it. But there's also a chance you may never see it again."

"Never . . ." Distress furrowed her brow. "But you don't understand, that car means a lot to me."

"There are other 450SLs."

"Maybe, but this one was a gift from my father." Unexpectedly, pain darkened her eyes—this close he could see they were an entrancing shade of hazel. She bit her lower lip, as if she were afraid it would quiver. "He gave it to me just before he died."

Compassion seized Mark, making him wonder what she'd do if he gathered her into his arms to offer comfort. She suddenly looked so vulnerable standing there, chewing on that delectable lip. "I'm sorry about your father," he said awkwardly. *But I'm even sorrier about never getting a chance to taste that sweet mouth of yours.* He saw her stiffen and for one wild moment imagined she'd read his mind.

But then her mouth firmed stubbornly. "Save your apologies. They're about as useful to me as this city's police department. I guess I'll just have to find my car myself."

Mark wearily rubbed a hand down his face. "I wouldn't advise that. You're liable to find yourself in a worse scrape than the one you had tonight." He reached into his back pocket for his wallet, pulled out one of his business cards and handed it to her. "This has my home and office numbers. Call me before you do anything rash."

She gave the card a disdainful glance. "I can take care of myself. Good night, Sergeant Sampson."

Repressing an urge to tell her what he thought of her ability to take care of herself, Mark muttered, "Good night," and stepped outside. He winced slightly when the door banged shut behind him.

BUT I'M EVEN SORRIER *about never getting a chance to kiss that sweet mouth of yours.* The words echoed in Sheri's mind as she contemplated the silk-draped canopy of her water bed hours later. She could no longer deny the source of the message, but that didn't mean she liked the idea of thought sharing, perceiving the innermost workings of another person's mind. The intimacy of it made her shift uneasily against the warm satin of the sheets. Having it happen with Mark Sampson left her feeling invaded, and the invasion wasn't restricted to her mind.

Sheri groaned, remembering the exquisite detail of that lovemaking fantasy. How long had it been since she'd felt that wild stirring in her blood? Restlessly she flopped over and onto her other side, hugging a pillow as she tried to remember. With Carlo, yes, but that had been the first hot rush of puberty, where sampling the forbidden had been a good portion of the thrill.

Certainly not in her marriage. Even in the beginning, Everett had concentrated on turning her into an acceptable banker's wife. He'd always given her the impression he found unbridled passion a little distasteful—in addition to her circus background.

Sheri sat up so quickly, the water-filled mattress rippled beneath her. She'd been married to a man who couldn't accept her for what she was, so how could she possibly feel any attraction to Mark Sampson when he obviously felt the same way?

Therein lay the truly aggravating aspect of the whole business. As ill-suited as they seemed to be, how could there be this intimate communication between their minds? She certainly hadn't asked for it.

"Why couldn't you keep your sexy thoughts to yourself, Sergeant Sampson?" Tossing the covers aside, she scrambled off the bed and stamped out to the kitchen to try the soporific effect of a glass of warm milk.

An hour later she was just slipping into a pleasant doze when the telephone beside her bed rang. Half-asleep, she raised the receiver to her ear and muttered, "Hello?" She repeated herself several times before she realized there wasn't going to be any response. Swearing softly, she hung up, buried her head under the pillow and groaned. First her car, then Sergeant

Sampson. *Now some nutzo decides to call.* . . . It certainly hadn't been one of her better evenings.

BRIGHT SUNSHINE backlighted the few clouds left over from the previous night as Mark Sampson ushered his daughter out the door of their pleasant ranch-style home.

"Hey, Dad! Look, I can see my breath!" April announced, huffing out more air to watch it condense in the chilly atmosphere.

"That's great, but we have to hurry." He tried not to show his impatience as he urged her toward the Bronco. Most mornings he allowed time for a little of her dawdling, but today he'd overslept—the result of a restless night filled with too many lurid dreams. When he opened the vehicle's door, he received an unwelcome reminder of the source of those dreams.

"What's this?" April demanded, reaching past him to gather up the mass of slithery white material.

Mark sighed. "I think it's called a veil. Let me have it, please. We need to get moving so I can deliver these cookies to the kids who're supposed to distribute them."

April obediently handed the veil to him, but he knew he wasn't off the hook. Even the adorably oversize lenses of her glasses couldn't mask the avid gleam in her brown eyes. "Whose is it? How did it get here? It smells like perfume. Was it a lady?" began the rapid-fire interrogation. At eight, April already had the instincts of a paparazzo.

Wincing, Mark hustled her into the seat and got in himself before he gave in to the inevitable. "Yes, it belongs to a lady, her name is Sheri, and I gave her a ride home last night."

"Why? Was she pretty? Did you have a date with her? Can I meet her?"

"It wasn't a date. She . . . uh, danced at that party I had to go to last night. And no, you can't meet her, because I don't intend to see her again." The Bronco lurched a little as Mark backed out of the driveway and headed down the street.

"Why not?" April peered up into his face, leaning over as far as her seat belt would allow. The action brought her long brown hair forward over her shoulders in a smooth silken curtain. "Was she fat like Francine? You don't go out with her anymore."

"Francine isn't fat," Mark corrected, biting back an urge to laugh.

"Her top is."

A dry chuckle escaped him. "Uh, most people don't consider that as being fat. Look, Munchkin, I'll be straight with you. I didn't get along too well with the lady last night." *Except in your fantasies*, his conscience accused.

"Does that mean I can keep the veil? Please, Dad, can I?" Her beseeching look reminded him sharply of how much she resembled her mother. The classic oval shape of her face, the slightly tip-tilted nose, even her coloring was a carbon copy of Melanie's. Fortunately for him, some roll of the genetic dice had blessed her with a temperament closer to his pragmatism than Melanie's quixotic disposition. Although there were times . . .

"Please, Dad?" April repeated, bringing him back to the question at hand.

"Sorry, honey. I'm sure the lady will want it back as soon as possible." *So she can practice her wiles on some other poor unsuspecting male.* His mood took a nosedive, and April didn't help matters when she flopped back into her seat with a petulant scowl.

LATER THAT MORNING, Mark pulled open the side drawer of his desk for what must have been the tenth time and scowled down at the filmy mass of white material lying inside. He nearly fell out of his chair when Lou's voice unexpectedly came from behind.

"A souvenir from last night? Damn, you work fast, gringo." Lou's black eyes were alight with mischief as he plunked a disposable cup down on the desk and took the free chair in Mark's cubicle-type office.

"Not even close." Mark glared at him, slammed the drawer shut and gestured toward the cup. "What's this, a bribe to make me forget your involvement in last night's fiasco?"

"Nope, it's from Sheri. I happened to stop by her place this morning and she asked me to bring it to you. Said something about broadening your outlook."

Mark froze in the act of prying the lid off the cup. "You went to her house this morning?"

Lou chuckled. "Do I detect a note of jealousy in that question? No, don't get mad again. I went to her shop. She owns a place called Café Gourmet in the Kensington area—not far from your house, actually. Sells gourmet goodies, fancy coffees, stuff like that. The place is standing room only during the morning rush hour, and she has live jazz on Sunday nights."

Scheherazade O'Reilly owned a business? Another concept that didn't fit with his original impression of her. Although the part about jazz did. She probably had a bunch of weirdos hanging around all the time.

"I wanted to see how she was faring after all the excitement last night," Lou continued. He winked and nodded in the direction of the desk drawer. "Care to explain that?"

Mark finally got the lid off the coffee cup and caught a whiff of coffee laced with something spicy. Cinnamon? "She must have dropped it last night. I found it on the floor of the truck this morning."

He took a cautious sip of the coffee and made a face. It *was* cinnamon. He'd thought chocolate-almond flavoring a little odd, but what kind of flake put cinnamon in coffee?

"So when are you going to take the lady's costume back to her?" Lou inquired with feigned casualness.

"I though I might mail it."

"Tell me another one, pal. You're as attracted to her as she is to you. I could see it even when you two were sparring like alley cats last night."

Some recess of Mark's brain jerked to attention. Sheri attracted to him? She sure did a good job of hiding it. "You couldn't be more wrong," he said, placing the coffee cup on his desk with care. "She was ready to slug me by the time I'd told her I wasn't going to chase all over the city looking for her car. Aside from that, she's not my type. You of all people should know how I feel about dancers."

"Not every dancer is like your ex-wife," Lou said, suddenly sober. "I'll admit Melanie did a number on you, but that was years ago. Besides, from what my sister has to say, Sheri isn't that type at all. Despite her rather flamboyant style, the lady has both feet planted firmly on the ground."

"She's still not my type." Mark took another sip of coffee and pushed the cup away in disgust. "Anyone who'd put cinnamon in coffee should be taken out and shot."

Lou sighed in defeat and got up to leave. "Have it your way. But I think you're making a big mistake. Sheri looked like she'd make a real nice armful."

Growling in incoherent response, Mark grabbed a file off his desk and made a show of reading it until Lou left. Only then did he allow himself to pull open the drawer and lift the soft mass of material to his nose. Her scent was there, reaching out to allure him as she had the night before. Cursing softly, he tossed the veil back into the drawer and shoved it closed. Then, for good measure, he downed the cup of hot coffee in one long punishing drink.

SHERI STUCK HER HANDS into the pockets of her rust suede slacks and surveyed Café Gourmet's late-afternoon crowd with a quiet sigh of relief. Business had been hectic for most of the day, instead of just in the morning. Now, however, there were only a few of the regulars scattered among the carved wooden booths and bentwood tables and chairs. Maybe she could catch up on the inventory check she'd started earlier in the week. The low heels of her shoes tapped smartly on the highly polished wooden floor as she crossed to the long counter where her brother Sean sat reading a book.

"Hey, Einstein." She squeezed his shoulder lightly. "I think it's time to give a little attention to the flora in this place."

Sean looked up at her with the slightly dazed expression he always got when he'd been buried in one of his technical tomes. "Huh? Oh, right, the plants." His hazel eyes, almost identical to her own, began to focus. "Just let me finish this chapter."

Sheri shook her head. "Uh-uh, if I do, you'll forget." She indicated the lush foliage of the numerous plants decorating the room, some hanging from the ceiling, others nestled in brightly painted pots. "The plants are alive, or at least they are right now." Her hand came around to rap on the cover of his book. "I'm willing to bet the guy who wrote this isn't."

Sean gave her a despairing look, but put the book aside and got up. Standing, he was six inches taller than her five and a half feet. His hair leaned more toward auburn than hers, and his handsome features were uncompromisingly masculine, but unlike some fraternal twins, he bore a striking resemblance to his sister.

"Come on, I can't reach the hanging plants without the ladder, and it'll only take you a few minutes." She patted his shoulder before adding, "And don't forget you have a class tonight. You should leave here by five." Her brother might have an IQ that topped hers by a healthy margin, but he tended to forget things, like the courses he taught at a local drama school or where he'd parked his car.

"You're such a nag," Sean complained, a spark of mischief in his eyes. "What you need is a husband to pick on."

Sheri took a playful swing at him, but he ducked and did a beautifully orchestrated, slow-motion fall to the floor, which was followed by a silent comic opera of a man in the throes of death.

Standing over him, Sheri didn't know whether to laugh or sigh in regret. The man sprawled before her had more college degrees than the average nuclear scientist, had been wooed by the nation's foremost research labs and earned more money than some men saw in a lifetime during his short career in the commercial world. Yet two years ago, at the ripe old age of thirty, he'd walked away from it without a backward glance. And all because of a garrulous old woman who'd tried too hard to order the lives of others.

Sean's thick fringe of eyelashes fluttered, betraying his covert perusal, and Sheri obediently offered silent applause. *Congratulations, Grandmother,* she thought sadly. *You managed to produce the exact opposite of what you wanted, both in your son and in Sean.*

Apparently satisfied with Sheri's response to his performance, Sean vaulted upright and snapped her a stiff salute, then goose-stepped into the back room where the watering can was kept.

Watching him go, Sheri couldn't help but wonder what would have happened if Grandmother O'Reilly hadn't been so determined to take them out of "that degenerate environment," as she'd called the circus. Sean certainly wouldn't have been shipped off to an elite private school back East, while Sheri had plodded through San Diego's public-school system.

That had been the most horrible part, being separated from him after twelve years of almost constant companionship. And even though they'd seen each other on vacations and occasional holidays, the special nature of their twinship had never been the same. Sean had withdrawn more and more into his solitary world of academia, ultimately putting an end to the silent communication they'd shared as children.

Even after Grandmother's death, when he'd returned to San Diego, claiming a need to reestablish family ties, a certain degree of distance had remained. Sheri knew he loved her as much as she loved him, but all communication between them took place on a verbal level now.

Which brought her back to the question that had been bothering her since last night. Why the mind-reading experience with Mark Sampson, when she couldn't even manage it with her brother, who at least cared for her?

"You may never know the answer to that one," she muttered to herself, rolling up the silky sleeves of her bright yellow shirt. For now she'd stick to something easy and mundane, like inventory.

A while later, perched atop the ladder in the back room, Sheri heard the musical jingle of the bells over the front entry. Checking her watch, she noted she had a few more minutes before Sean left, and went back to counting boxes of imported Scottish shortbread. Engrossed in the task, she had no idea she was no longer alone until a low, rasping voice asked, "Do you make a habit of risking your neck?"

Startled, Sheri twisted around, lost her precarious balance and tumbled backward. Instead of the hard floor, however, she felt herself land in a pair of muscular arms, which in turn hugged her to a broad hard chest. Her breath puffed out in a startled "Oh!" as she found her arms wrapping themselves around her rescuer's neck. When she looked up at his face, she encountered Mark Sampson's stunning blue eyes. Without warning, something warm and intimate swept through her. Like a mental caress, she thought, dazed.

Their faces were so close, she could feel the hot, moist gust of his breath as he recovered from the exertion of catching her. And the warm sensation deepened to a heated thrill when she realized he was just one breath away from kissing her. Caught in the inevitability of the moment, she cried out in surprise when the support of his arms suddenly gave way and she found herself on her feet.

She stumbled backward and crashed into a wall of shelves containing jars of imported jams. By some miracle, none fell to the floor, but that didn't lessen Sheri's sense of outrage. She glared at him and demanded, "Do you make a *habit* of sneaking up on people and scaring them half to death?"

Mark hesitated, visibly controlling his own temper before answering. "No. I found this in my truck and thought you might like to have it back." He held out a brown paper bag.

Wary, Sheri accepted it and peered inside. "My veil! So that's what happened to it."

"Sis?" The sound of Sean's voice pulled her attention to the doorway. Her brother stood there, his dark eyes unusually alert as he viewed the vignette before him. "Is everything all right? I thought I heard someone yell."

"Everything is just great," Sheri assured him quickly as she ran a hand over her tousled hair. Could Sean sense the afterbeat of passion in the air? She didn't relish the idea of him being able to read her mind at this particular moment. Things were complicated enough.

"She fell off the ladder and would have broken her neck if I hadn't caught her," Mark put in sternly.

Sean frowned. "I keep telling her she's too careless when she uses that thing."

"Now just a minute," Sheri interjected. "I wouldn't have fallen off the ladder if you hadn't sneaked up on me, Sergeant Sampson. And as for you—" she turned on her brother "—you might be the twin with the higher IQ, but when it comes to physical coordination, we're equals."

Sean opened his mouth as if to respond, but Mark spoke first. "I didn't sneak. And furthermore, I'm getting pretty tired of hearing you yell at me every time I rescue you."

"You mean there's been more than one?" Sean looked intrigued. "By the way, I'm Sean, Sheri's brother." He advanced farther into the room to shake hands with Mark and added with a grin, "The smarter twin."

"This is Sergeant Sampson," Sheri supplied reluctantly. "He was at the party last night when my car was stolen."

"The name's Mark. And what your sister forgot to mention is that I'm the one who kept her from being run over by said car."

"Damn it, Sheri. You didn't say anything about being in danger." Sean's normally benign features took on an appraising sharpness as he studied Mark.

Sheri didn't like that look at all and liked his next statement even less. "So you're in the habit of saving my sister, hmm?"

"I don't need anyone to save me!" Sheri nearly shouted, but took a step back when Sean turned on her with surprising vehemence.

"You do if you keep taking crazy risks." He pointed to the ten-speed bicycle propped in a back corner of the room. "Like riding that thing home after dark. I still think you should wait until I can pick you up tonight."

"We settled that this morning. The bike has a light and it's only eight blocks to my house. I'm not going to sit around here until ten o'clock when I could be home working. I have to make French pastries tonight so they'll be ready in the morning." She glanced pointedly at her watch. "Speaking of work, you're going to be late for your class again if you don't get moving."

"In other words, I'm dismissed." Sean shook his head and turned to Mark. "Nice meeting you. I'd appreciate it if you'd talk some sense into her. You look like you might be able to pull it off."

When Sean had disappeared into the front of the store, Mark turned back to Sheri. "He's right, you know. Riding around after dark isn't a good idea, even in a quiet neighborhood like this one."

"I never even considered the idea before my car was stolen," she shot back. "And since *I* haven't had time to start looking for it yet . . ."

"You aren't really serious about doing that, are you?" Mark's neck began to turn a telltale red beneath the crisp collar of his blue-and-white-striped shirt.

He looked as if he was preparing to deliver another lecture on her habits, so she decided not to answer. Instead she shrugged noncommittally and headed past him toward the front of her shop. "You'll have to excuse me. I have a business to run."

She could hear Mark muttering as he followed, and opted for the safety zone behind her long service counter. He moved to face her from the other side, but before either of them could speak, the electronic pager at his belt sent out a shrill summons. Glad of the interruption, she offered the use of her telephone, and while he called in, she hurried to prepare a package of freshly ground coffee for him.

When he returned from using the telephone in the back, she held out a white paper bag bearing Café Gourmet's insignia. "Just a little something to show my appreciation for...er, your help last night. It's medium grind, so you can use any kind of coffee maker." She didn't mention the coffee was Jamaican Blue Mountain, which sold for thirty dollars a pound.

Mark looked embarrassed as he accepted the sack. "You didn't have to—"

"Yes, I did," she interrupted. "I know it isn't enough payment for having my life saved, but I want to do something." She waved a hand toward the display cases holding various confections and baked goods. "If there's anything else you'd like . . ."

"No, nothing." He grinned suddenly. "You're dismissing me, aren't you? Just like you brushed off your brother."

Sheri displayed her most dazzling smile. "I'm not dismissing you, I'm just . . . releasing you from your responsibility for me."

Mark eyed her for a moment, then glanced around the room, taking in the fanciful decor. Circus posters, like the ones in her home, graced the walls, along with a veritable jungle of exotic plants. On the far side the rest-room doors had elaborate, gilt-edged signs bearing the legends Gentlemen and Ladies. And in one corner a scarlet-and-gold banner announced Madame Zola—Psychic Readings.

"Do you believe in that stuff?" he inquired, indicating the banner with a jerk of his head.

You don't know the half of it, my friend, Sheri thought. Since she didn't intend to enlighten him, she smiled and said, "Depends on the circumstances. I've had enough carny experience to recognize most frauds."

"What about this Madame Zola?"

Her smile turned mysterious, but before she could respond, the door to the men's rest room opened and Sean appeared, dressed in his mime costume of black stretch overalls and black-and-white-striped knit shirt. His features were barely recognizable beneath a layer of white and black makeup.

The ensuing silence reminded Sheri of the dramatic pause that sometimes precedes the punch line of a good joke. Except the look on Mark's face didn't make her feel like laughing. After a long moment he turned to her and asked incredulously, "He's a mime?"

Regardless of her own feelings about her brother's career or lack of one, Sheri jumped to his defense. "How clever of you to notice," she retorted. "Do you find that objectionable?"

Before Mark could answer, Sean intervened, crossing the room to offer Mark a handshake and a formal little bow. Then Sheri found herself wrapped in her brother's strong young arms as he pretended to smother her with affectionate kisses. "Goodbye, crazy person," she said with a giggle, unable to remain angry in the face of his silliness.

When he had gone, Mark cleared his throat uneasily. "Is that what he does for a living?"

This time Sheri managed to keep her temper in check. After all, she didn't owe Mark Sampson any explanations. "My brother and I have many talents," she said, "one of which is surviving quite nicely without conforming to other people's standards."

As if she'd been summoned to prove a point, Madame Zola chose that moment to come sweeping through the front door to the accompanying jingle of the bells hung over it. Dressed in her "working clothes," as she called them, she resembled a rotund Gypsy woman gone Hollywood. After a bright,

"Hello, deary," aimed at Sheri, the woman proceeded to the banner-strung corner and settled herself at the table there.

Mark shook his head and looked at Sheri. He started to say something, then checked himself and strolled toward the door. Just before closing it behind him, he turned and said, "You don't have to say it—I know it's none of my business. But do me a favor. Quit risking that pretty neck of yours. I might not be around to save it next time."

The jingling bells cut off Sheri's retort. "Just as well," she muttered, moving to offer assistance to Madame Zola. "I won't be seeing him again anyway. Not after today."

Later that evening she couldn't help feeling a little surge of defiance as she wheeled her bicycle out the back door of the shop. Men! They were always so eager to tell a woman how helpless she was without them.

She locked the door and turned toward the bike, feeling courageous and determined. Her bravado vanished when a large shadow suddenly detached itself from the blackness at the back of the building and loomed over her. Shoving the bike aside, she started to run, but her assailant was too quick. Next thing she knew, she was struggling against a terribly strong pair of arms and her scream was being muffled by a solid, leather-clad chest. She'd nearly succeeded in a knee-to-the-groin movement when a familiar voice grated in her ear.

"Sheri...ouch! Blast it, quit fighting. It's me, Mark Sampson."

3

SHERI'S FEAR turned to indignation and, instead of ceasing, her struggles intensified.

"Sheri . . . ow! . . . damn it, that was my shin!"

For a moment, wicked satisfaction danced through her at the idea of holding her own against him. But Mark's years as a police officer gave him a distinct advantage. In the next instant she found herself up against the wall of the building, held immobile by his lean tough body. Her hands were pinned by his on either side of her head, and while he wasn't actually hurting her, the restraint was demoralizing. Tilting her head back, she glared at him. "What are you doing here?"

"I came to offer you a ride home," Mark responded a bit breathlessly.

"Why? I released you from any further responsibility this afternoon." She squirmed a little beneath the weight of his body, not from discomfort, but from the sudden awareness of how good it felt. Her breasts were pressed hard against the firm muscles of his chest, and with each breath their torsos came together in a way that made her shiver inside.

"I know you dismissed me, but . . ." Mark let out a deep sigh. "For some crazy reason I find myself caring about what happens to you." He glanced downward, as if just then sensing the intimate contact of their bodies. When he looked up again, his eyes were dark with awakening desire.

It took only the slightest movement of his head to bring their mouths together, and from the first touch of his warm firm lips she was lost. His mouth opened over hers in hungry demand, and her entire being responded to the need to satisfy him. With only the smallest hesitation she gave in to the nudge of his tongue and let him take the kiss to even greater depths. He tasted wonderful. And he knew how to play wicked little games with that tongue, enticing and twining and stroking until she felt she would go mad.

Glorious, transcendent sensation drew Sheri deeper and deeper, wiping out reason and conscious thought. She nearly cried out in dismay when Mark drew his head back sharply, released a long, frustrated breath and stepped away from her.

"This is crazy," he muttered. "I came here to offer you a ride home, nothing more."

Sheri felt like hitting him again. "Then why did you kiss me like that?"

Because I haven't been able to think of anything else since this afternoon. The phrase seemed to echo in the silence of the quiet side street.

Sheri opened her mouth to respond to his comment, then shut it quickly when the truth hit her. He hadn't spoken aloud. Good grief, it had happened again.

Obviously unaware of having revealed himself, Mark gave her a sardonic look. "I don't suppose you'd believe me if I said I was trying to keep you from bringing down the whole neighborhood with your screams."

"I never had any intention of screaming."

Mark snorted. "Oh, come on, admit it. For a minute there you were scared." Without waiting for an answer, he picked up her fallen bicycle and started wheeling it toward his truck, which was parked across the street.

"I wouldn't have been scared if you hadn't jumped out at me," she insisted stubbornly. Given no other choice, she followed him across the street, zipping up the front of her hot-pink windbreaker as she went. If anything, the air was colder than the night before, and a ride home in a warm vehicle sounded awfully attractive, even if she was irritated with the driver.

"Consider yourself lucky it was me and not the thug I saw loitering on the corner across from your store."

An uneasy sensation swept over Sheri. "What thug? I didn't see anyone."

"That's because he left when I arrived."

She shrugged, wanting to be free of the sinister feeling his suggestion had caused. "If it had been some thug instead of you, I would've succeeded with my second knee-to-the, uh, privates."

"You came close enough," Mark said dryly. He stowed the bicycle in the back of the Bronco and closed the door. As he turned to her, he gingerly rubbed his right hand over the front of one thigh. "Where did you learn to fight like that?"

"From a police officer," she told him with great relish. "I took a class in self-defense at night school."

The amber glow of a nearby street lamp intensified the sharp planes of Mark's face as he frowned. "And now you think you're invincible." He opened the passenger door and motioned her inside.

"No, I don't. But I have been taking care of myself for a long time." She considered refusing to climb up into the inviting warmth of the front seat, but was too cold to resist.

"You really should wear a decent coat on a night like this," Mark advised, his hand unnecessarily clasping her elbow to help her up.

Sheri had to save her rejoinder, because he shut the door, cutting her off. But as soon as he got in, she said, "At the moment I don't possess a decent coat. It's lying in the back seat of my car, which is also no longer in my possession."

"That figures," Mark muttered, shrugging out of his jacket. But his attitude changed when she rejected the offered garment. "Look, I'm really sorry about your coat—and your car. I've even done what I can to see that you get them back. Everyone in my division and Lou's has been asked to be on the lookout when they're in the field. If anything turns up, I intend to check it out personally."

His admission surprised her so much, she stopped trying to evade his efforts to drape the jacket over her shoulders. Once again the warmth and scent of Mark Sampson enveloped her, and she nearly gave in to a contented sigh.

"I thought you didn't trouble yourself with unimportant cases like mine," she said, wanting to dispel the returning wave of physical attraction that was threatening her objectivity. After all, the man still disapproved of her. His next words merely served to reinforce that fact.

"Normally I wouldn't. But I hate to think of what might happen to you if you decided to start your own investigation."

"Meaning I need to be protected from myself. Gee, thanks." Sheri turned to glare out the windshield.

The Bronco's engine roared to life, and a disgruntled silence settled over them as it had on their previous trip to her home. Mark pulled into her driveway and killed the engine, before angling around in his seat to face her. "I didn't mean that as an insult," he said in a low voice. "I was trying to tell you that I care about your safety. Why do you misinterpret everything I say?"

"For the same reason you misinterpret everything I do." Sheri turned to look at him. "Our personalities are direct opposites. We have absolutely nothing in common." What she couldn't figure out was, why did the admission distress her so?

"I think you're wrong. There is one thing." Without warning he reached for a lock of her hair and rubbed it between his fingers, like a man savoring the texture of fine silk. A simple gesture, but with it came a pulsing sensuality that seemed to fill the confined space they shared.

"I have a confession to make." His voice had developed a dreamy huskiness. "When I kissed you back there, I did it because I'd been thinking about it ever since this afternoon."

"I know." What she didn't say was how she had come to know. She could just imagine his reaction if she told him about her intermittent ability to read his mind. As it was, he thought little enough of her mental stability. Knowing that made her tug the strand of hair out of his fingers with a little twist of her head. "The fact remains, we don't match."

This time the heat in Mark's voice wasn't entirely sensual. "Look, I'll admit you're not the kind of woman I normally see, but I thought we could . . ."

Hurt and rage boiled up inside Sheri with volcanic force. "I get it. Nothing serious, just go for the gusto, right? In other words, I'm not good enough for a real relationship. Well, get this. I don't waste my time on self-righteous stuffed shirts." She wrenched the door open and tried to jump out, but he caught her from behind and hauled her back.

"Not so fast," he snapped. "What made you think I meant you weren't good enough for me?"

Twisting furiously in the unrelenting grip of his hands, Sheri snapped right back, "Because I've heard the line before. Unfortunately I was married to the last guy who felt compelled to tell me."

Mark's expression tightened and he gave her a little shake. "Then get ready for an update. I'm not that other guy. And I wasn't putting you down. Once again you've jumped to the wrong conclusion."

She stilled. "Like you did last night when you saw me dance."

"I thought I apologized for that."

"Maybe, but you still think less of me for doing it."

"Not for the reason you're assuming. You don't have a monopoly on hurt, you know."

Sheri detected the pain in his harsh revelation, but steeled herself against the flash of empathy in her heart. "Then let's not hurt each other anymore. As soon as you unload my bike, you can be on your way."

He looked as though he might be ready to argue, but then sighed and said, "Maybe you're right."

After wheeling her bicycle to the front porch, he watched as she chained it to the iron railing. "At least tell me you won't try riding that thing home at night."

Sheri tested the chain with a little tug, then rose to face him. "Don't worry. Sean called me a while ago. He was able to arrange a ride to work with a friend, so I can use his car." She slipped off his jacket and handed it to him. "Thanks again for the ride."

"Think nothing of it." He slung the jacket over his shoulder, holding it with one curled finger. But he didn't leave until she'd unlocked the front door and slipped inside.

Sheri leaned back against the closed door until she heard the Bronco's powerful engine rumble to life, then an irresistible urge made her race to her bedroom window to watch the vehicle back out of the driveway and disappear down the street. When it was out of sight, a strange despondency settled over her.

"It's too bad you weren't my type, Sergeant Mark Sampson," she murmured, letting the curtain fall back into place. "You're the best kisser I've ever known."

For just a moment she pressed her fingertips to her lips, then straightened her spine and headed for the kitchen. Several hours of baking still awaited her if she wanted to keep the shelves in her pastry display stocked. She had enough problems in her life without taking on one like Mark Sampson.

A WEEK PASSED, and Sheri had begun to think her life had settled back into its normal rhythm, when the telephone calls began. The first came early one evening, and Sheri absently reached for the receiver as she tried to finish one last sentence in the thriller she was reading. Following her hello there was no response, just the ominous sound of heavy breathing. A quick stab of fear threatened her momentarily, but she refused to give in to it. She simply hung up. After all, it had worked the night her car was stolen.

To her dismay the calls continued, one per night, usually in the mid-to-late evening, and when several days had passed, her patience began to wear thin. She tried saying things like "Sorry, wrong number," or "You really should do something about that asthma," before she hung up. That didn't work, either. After a week her temper won out.

She'd just set the receiver back in its cradle one night—there'd been another of the annoying calls—when the instrument rang again. Yanking the receiver back to her ear, she shouted, "All right you lousy son of a—!"

Mark Sampson's astonished voice cut her off. "Sheri? Is that you?"

Mortified, she covered her eyes and mumbled, "Uh, yes."

Mark chuckled. "I didn't expect you to be overjoyed to hear from me, but I think that greeting was a little extreme. By the way, how did you know it was me? Are you a clairvoyant, in addition to all your other talents?"

You don't want to know the answer to that one, Sheri thought. "I wasn't expecting you," she said aloud. "I've been getting some breather phone calls, and I decided to give the guy a piece of my mind."

"Breather calls?" Mark's voice sharpened. "How long has this been going on?"

"About a week. It's mostly a nuisance."

"Have you reported it to the phone company?"

"Yes. They wanted me to change my number, which I can't do because of the business calls I get. And the guy doesn't stay on the line long enough to allow tracing. So I'm, uh, dealing with it in my own manner."

"I noticed. Has he ever referred to you by name?"

"No. I doubt that he knows it, unless he's a customer or something. I'm listed under an initial in the directory, with no address." Sheri experienced a little twist of anxiety. Why did he sound so concerned?

"Did you ever consider that the man who stole your car might have access to personal information about you? Your registration was in the glove box, right?"

The implication behind his query heightened her unease. "Exactly what are you suggesting?"

"I'm not suggesting anything. I'm only urging you to use caution. This city has its share of crazies."

"Tell me something I don't know," Sheri drawled. The conversation was beginning to sound like a lecture, one she'd already heard from him. "Was there any other reason for your call?"

Yeah. I couldn't go another day without hearing your voice.

His silent message caused such a pounding in her heart, she nearly missed his audible answer.

"I, um, thought you might like to know we're investigating rumors of several car-theft rings that specialize in foreign cars like yours."

Still caught up in the power of his unspoken admission, Sheri struggled for something to say. "Oh. Well . . . that's great, I guess. Thank you."

"No thanks necessary. It's just part of my job."

An awkward pause ensued, more like that between two adolescents than two experienced adults. Sheri couldn't keep the amusement from her voice as she asked, "Was there anything else? Or were you waiting for a turn to breathe in my ear?"

Mark laughed softly. "Not really. But I would like for you to call me right away if your breather starts talking, especially if he refers to you by name."

Sheri rolled her eyes. There he went with that alarmist attitude again. "I don't expect that to happen—"

Mark cut in roughly. "Just humor me and say you will, okay?"

"Fine, you'll be the second to know, Sergeant Sampson." Stalemate again, Sheri noted ruefully as she hung up. But she couldn't forget Mark's real reason for calling. He'd wanted to hear her voice. To be absolutely honest, she'd welcomed the sound of his. And the telepathy had felt different this time, less of an intrusion. No, more than that, she amended. It had been marvelous, experiencing the sharp longing in him—a longing like the one she kept trying to deny her own heart.

Just admitting it agitated her. She got up from the couch and went to the corner where her little horse danced in splendor. "You and I will be the only ones who ever know it," she muttered, stroking the sculpted wave of his mane.

"Are you going to tell me what's bothering you, or do I have to guess?" Sean's unexpected question made Sheri straighten in surprise. They'd been rearranging furniture to make room for the belly-dancing class she held after-hours at Café Gourmet.

"Nothing's bothering me," she replied carefully. Had she been that transparent? "What makes you think there is?"

"Oh, come on, Sis. I might not be able to read your mind anymore, but I can see what's right before my eyes. You look like you're auditioning for the role of Camille. It's that cop, isn't it?"

Sheri turned from shoving a stack of chairs and stared at him. "How did you come to that conclusion?"

Sean grinned. "Simple deduction, my dear Watson. *A*—you haven't been dating lately. And *B*—I witnessed that electric little moment you shared with him in the back room. The chemistry in there was more powerful than atomic energy." He narrowed his eyes. "Is there some kind of connection between you two?"

Sheri busied herself moving a table away from the mirrored wall that ran the length of the room. "I'm not seeing him, if that's what you mean."

"No, I was referring to something a little more ethereal." He blocked her attempt to dodge around him and gently placed his hands upon her shoulders. When she looked into his eyes, she felt a brief spark of their old closeness.

"How did you know?" she inquired, frowning up at him.

"I don't. Not exactly. Why don't you tell me about it?"

She shrugged and looked away. "There isn't much to tell. I just . . . a few times I picked up what he was thinking. It doesn't make sense, really. I hardly know the man, and he irritates me more than anything else."

Almost anything.

"But you can't forget him." Sean released her and shoved his hands into the pockets of his navy slacks. "Maybe there's more to this than you realize. After all, there is a history of telepathic ability on the maternal side of our family, Great-aunt Isabella, for one, and you and I being the most recent. And remember how Lila always claimed she'd been able to read our father's thoughts while they were together? She said it was a sign of destiny."

Sheri raised an eyebrow at his use of their mother's first name, but didn't bother to call him on it. Heaven only knows, their mother hadn't done much to inspire maternal images. "Our parents' relationship didn't exactly work out. Mental communion couldn't counteract our father's aversion to responsibility and permanent ties. Even if it had, to suggest that Mark and I are destined for each other is pretty farfetched." She shook her head dismissively and started toward the last group of chairs.

"Stranger things have happened," Sean insisted, following her. When the main portion of the floor was clear he tried again. "So what are you going to do about the man?"

Sheri gestured impatiently. "Nothing! Beyond forgetting him, that is. I figure it's only a matter of time." When Sean looked doubtful she added, "I'll be fine, honest."

ACROSS THE STREET, Denny Plover watched the scene taking place behind the windows of Café Gourmet and wondered what was going on. He uttered a low grunt of frustration when the woman drew the café curtains, cutting off his view. It was *her*—the one who'd tried to stop him when he'd stolen her car. That he knew for certain. A guy didn't forget the face of a goddess, even if he got only a brief glance. And she had looked like a goddess, dressed in all that white swirly stuff. Too beautiful for words.

Too beautiful for you, an inner voice sneered. Denny scowled unhappily and hunched his burly shoulders inside the heavy denim of his extralarge jacket. He knew he was no prize. His own mother had told him that often enough. "You're almost as slow and clumsy as you are big," she'd say. Or, "No use setting your heart on no pretty girl, not with that face of yours."

But a guy could look, couldn't he? And maybe he'd call her again, just to hear the sweet lilt in her voice when she said hello. Nah, he'd better cool it on the calls, she'd begun to sound mad on the last few. Besides, Luther said the cops could trace 'em real fast nowadays.

A slight commotion across the street caught Denny's attention. Several cars were now parked in front of the store and a group of women was filing inside, laughing and chattering excitedly. Stealthily he moved to a place on the sidewalk a few feet from the storefront. To his delight, he discovered his unusual height allowed him to look through the gap between the top and bottom curtains.

The women were all lined up, facing a mirrored wall where *she* stood. Sheri—Scheherazade. He'd learned her name from the pictures and papers he'd found in the car. He watched the dancers begin to sway to and fro, following Sheri's lead, some with grace, others with awkward determination. Denny's breathing became shallow and his mouth sagged open. So beautiful . . . so beautiful. . . .

A movement at the door shattered his reverie. The man he'd seen earlier was exiting, waving goodbye over his shoulder, promising to return in a while. Denny stumbled back into the shadows of a nearby storefront, nearly tripping over his own size fourteen feet. Breathlessly he waited, his heart thudding, until the man climbed into a car and drove off.

Her boyfriend, Denny surmised morosely. *What chance does a guy like me have against a smooth dude like him? Man, he's got it all, and I got nothin'.* Except . . .

Denny felt the spark of an idea flicker to life. Her car. Maybe she'd be interested in getting that little red sports car back. She'd certainly looked ready to go to any length to stop him the night he'd stolen it.

Denny had one last look at the tantalizing sight beyond those curtains, then trudged off down the street to where he'd hidden the Mercedes. As he started it up and listened to the contented purr of the engine, a slow smile creased his thick features. Maybe there was a way....

THE CHEERFUL CHAOS of Café Gourmet's Saturday-morning crowd always lifted Sheri's spirits. Her shop had become a weekend meeting place for a lot of the local residents, and a pleasant sense of camaraderie reigned.

She'd just started to tell herself how great life was when her best friend Tina Reyes leaned over the service counter and announced, "You look a little ragged around the edges to me. Which is it, the flu or a man?"

Instantly the image of a lean angular face and sharp blue eyes flashed into Sheri's mind, startling her into guilty laughter. "Must be the flu," she said quickly. "You know I don't have time for dating."

"You could make time for the right guy." Tina's dark eyes narrowed shrewdly. "Lou seems to think there could be something between you and Mark Sampson."

At the mere mention of Mark's name, Sheri felt a little jump in her pulse. "Ridiculous," she muttered.

"What did you say?"

"I said anything between Mark Sampson and me would be ridiculous. We did nothing but fight the few times fate threw us together."

"So? My parents fight like cats and dogs sometimes, and they've been happily married for nearly forty years. The trick is learning to make up."

"You're sniffing down a cold trail," Sheri advised flatly. "I haven't seen the man for three weeks." Three weeks since that one unforgettable kiss. She pushed the thought away and busied herself waiting on a young couple who were gently haggling over what flavor coffee beans they wanted to try. When she returned to the front counter, she discovered Sean had been roped into the conversation.

"We've decided you need a little time off," Tina announced. "Sean's agreed to watch the store while I take you to lunch."

"You do look as though you could use a break, Sis," Sean put in obligingly. He nodded toward the teenagers waiting on tables, a pair of high schoolers who worked after school and on weekends. "The girls and I can handle things here after the morning rush."

"I'm not sick, and I'm not pining from lack of male companionship," Sheri insisted.

"Then consider this health insurance." Tina caught hold of her hand and tugged lightly. "Come on, it'll be great. We can go to Old Town and stuff ourselves with Mexican food and margaritas"

Sheri agreed, with the condition that they go in separate cars so she could return to work immediately afterward. Sean offered the use of his car, and Tina conceded after a disparaging remark about workaholics.

They arrived at the scenic older section of San Diego during the lunch-hour rush, which made locating parking spaces a challenge. But as they began to stroll among the graceful adobe buildings, Sheri's enthusiasm for the outing increased. The area was one of her favorites among San Diego's historic landmarks. They window-shopped among stores offering the colorful wares of Mexico and the handiwork of local artists. But before long the delicious aromas wafting from the area's wide assortment of restaurants proved irresistible.

By some stroke of luck, Tina managed to obtain an umbrella-shaded table in one of the patio dining spots. They ordered frosty green margaritas and chicken tostada salads. As soon as their drinks arrived, Tina revived the subject of Mark Sampson.

"So, what did you and Mark have to fight about?"

Sheri took a fortifying sip of her margarita, savoring the sting of lime, tequila and salt against her tongue. After a little hum of appreciation she said, "We disagreed on everything. You've heard the old line about opposites attract? Well, we didn't." *Except when he was kissing me—or telegraphing those X-rated thoughts of his.* A warm glow flared to life in the region of her stomach, but she stubbornly attributed it to the tequila.

Tina's black curls bounced as she shook her head regretfully. "Sounds like you really hate the guy."

"I didn't say that," Sheri hedged, unwilling to lie to her friend. The waiter arrived with their food, but as soon as he'd left, she attempted to end Tina's speculation once and for all. "Just forget any ideas you have about me and Sergeant Sampson. Even if I were interested—which I'm not—I'm sure he's forgotten me by now."

Tina quickly swallowed a bite of salad and grinned triumphantly. "Then why does he still have everyone he knows in the police department keeping an eye out for that little sports car of yours? Especially when he has to take lots of razzing about giving preferential treatment to belly dancers?"

"That's the crux of the problem." Sheri stabbed the air with her fork for emphasis. "He made it abundantly clear he didn't approve of my dancing—or my life-style. And I think he's far too conservative. We're a total mismatch personalitywise." Too bad she couldn't say the same for the physical side. She took a bite of spicy chicken and lettuce and chewed without tasting.

"Well, he is a little uptight about dancers," Tina admitted reluctantly. "But after the way his ex-wife treated him, it isn't hard to understand."

Sheri rolled her eyes. "Let me guess. She was a dancer. And what do you mean, 'ex'? He told me his wife was dead."

"She left him about a year before she died." Tina added a liberal portion of hot salsa to her salad. "I don't have all the details, Lou won't say much about it. But I do know Mark got burned. Evidently she'd been cheating on him for some time before she ran off to pursue her big career in New York. All she left Mark was a two-year-old daughter to raise and a bunch of bad memories."

"When did this happen?" Sheri asked, thinking of the Girl Scout cookies in Mark's Bronco that first night. His daughter had to be a lot older than two.

"Oh, years ago. April's eight now, and she's a super kid. Mark's done a fantastic job as a single parent, even if he is a little straitlaced at times." Tina sighed dramatically. "The only sad part is, he's never let another woman get close to him emotionally. I know, I went out with him once, and it was like dating a monk."

"Perhaps he's happy with that arrangement," Sheri suggested. To her irritation, she found the idea depressing. She didn't want to care about Mark Sampson's problems; her life was full enough already.

"That might have been true in the past, but I don't think it is any longer. According to Lou, Mark's changed lately. He seems restless, irritable." Tina paused and leaned forward with a significant look. "Like someone else I know."

"I have not been irritable," Sheri snapped, then grimaced. She had been peevish the past couple of weeks, she admitted grudgingly; it was a shortcoming she normally kept under control. Even Sean's innocuous foibles had begun to set her on edge.

"Let me put it this way," Tina said gently. "You haven't been your usual sunny self lately. And it seems like more than coincidence that Mark's been acting strangely, too. I haven't said anything, because you and I agreed long ago not to play matchmaker. But it sure sounds like something's going on."

"Okay, I'll admit there was some...physical attraction." Sheri poked at her salad. "Actually a lot. But that isn't enough for me, any more than it would be enough for you. So could we just drop the subject and enjoy our lunch?"

Tina looked as if she would have liked to argue, but finally agreed, and they turned to other topics for the rest of the meal.

On the ride back to her shop Sheri tried not to think about Mark Sampson, but the details of his marriage kept poking at her. It must have been tough for him and his little daughter, being deserted that way. Yet from what Tina said, April had come through it without noticeable harm. Picturing Mark in the role of a devoted father caused an odd stirring in Sheri's heart. Her own father had been conspicuous for his absence from her life and Sean's. The only tangible thing he'd left her was the dashing sports car he'd so cherished.

Two blocks later, almost as if it had been summoned by her thought, a bright red Mercedes 450SL zipped past, going in the other direction.

Sheri absently glanced into the rearview mirror for another look at the sports car. Amazing how much it looked like hers, even down to the funny little dent in the rear fender. Her eyes widened in recognition. "That's my car!"

The car tires squealed in protest as she stomped on the brakes and sharply jerked the steering wheel around to follow. Traffic screeched to a halt all around her and several horns blared angrily, but she didn't pay any attention. Nothing mattered but the disappearing bumper of that little red car. *Her car.* She was certain of it, even though the license plate was wrong. Frantic to catch up, she ground the gears on each shift, cruelly overrevving the engine. They were traveling through a residential area with narrow, winding streets that made real speed impossible. Even so, she had just begun to gain ground when her quarry seemed to sense her presence and increased his speed.

Knowing her brother's car couldn't possibly keep up if they reached a really straight stretch, Sheri swore in frustration. She needed help, but where was she going to find it in this sedate neighborhood?

The Mercedes took the next corner on two wheels, and she winced. On top of everything else, the fool was probably going to crash her car. She followed around the curve at a slightly saner pace and groaned when she saw the advantage the other car had gained. They had just crossed Washington Street when a flash of red in her rearview mirror caught her attention. Recognizing the distinctive black-and-white paint job of a police car, she let out a whoop of relief and waved frantically for them to follow.

Unfortunately the police officer had other ideas. He hit the siren, motioning for her to pull over. When that didn't work, he got onto his loudspeaker and ordered her to stop in no uncertain terms. Growling in frustration as she watched her Mercedes disappear around another corner, Sheri swerved to the curb and stopped.

4

SHE GOT OUT of the car and waited with foot-tapping impatience for the two slowly approaching officers. One was tall and athletically trim, the other shorter with a middle-aged paunch that distorted the crisp lines of his khaki uniform. The fact that they'd taken the precaution of carrying their riot batons didn't make her feel any better.

"Good afternoon, ma'am. May I see your driver's license?" It was the short one speaking, and she could see her own disgruntled expression reflected in his mirrored sunglasses.

"Yes, of course," she agreed irritably. "But you're letting the real criminal get away."

The two men glanced at each other, and the thin one asked, "Who might that be, ma'am?"

"The creep who stole my car, that's who." She handed over her license and suppressed an urge to tell them what she thought of the efficiency of their department in general.

"You say someone just stole your car," the heavier officer said with a nod toward Sean's VW. "Whose car is that?"

"My brother's," Sheri replied testily. "And I didn't say my car was just stolen. It happened three weeks ago."

This time the officers exchanged a more significant look, and the younger one spoke with studied courtesy. "I see. Could you give us the license number and a description of this car?"

"It's a red 450SL. And I can't remember the license number, because it wasn't mine."

"If it wasn't your license, how did you know it was your car?"

Sheri let out a sigh of exasperation. "Because it had a heart-shaped dent in the fender that I put there two days before it was stolen." The heavyset officer shifted his weight from one foot to the other, and she could see that he was biting his lip to keep from grinning. Overwhelmed by a need to establish her credibility, she snapped, "Look, if you don't believe me, contact Sergeant Mark Sampson. He's in charge of the auto-theft division in this city."

That seemed to get their attention, and for good measure she added, "He's personally involved in the case."

Mirror Eyes nodded obliquely to his partner and started back toward the patrol car. The other officer gestured toward the sidewalk. "Shall we wait over here, ma'am? My partner needs to verify your story, and I'd like to have you perform a few tests for me."

Sheri gritted her teeth and preceded him to the palm-lined walk. It was bad enough that they'd ruined her chance to reclaim her car. Now they were probably going to make her take a sobriety test.

MARK HAD JUST FINISHED setting out the third and final row of strawberry plants in his garden when his pager sounded. He got up and stretched, sighing as he surveyed the neat rows of lush greenery taking up half of his spacious backyard. He was used to getting calls from work on weekends, but he'd hoped to get a little more weeding done. At least he didn't have to worry about April; she was spending a couple of days with her grandparents. After a last regretful look at the unfinished garden, he headed for the house to call headquarters.

When the operator patched him through to a patrol car, the story he heard temporarily overrode his interest in gardening. "How fast did you say she was going?"

"We estimate about forty-five, tops. Normally we'd just cite her, but when she mentioned your personal involvement in the car theft, I thought I'd better check it out."

Personal involvement? Mark bit back a laugh. That only began to state the case. He hadn't laid eyes on the woman for three weeks, yet just hearing her name caused a surge of excitement in his blood. He'd tried everything he could think of to forget her, even to the extent of calling up a few old dates. Nothing had worked. He still thought of her constantly, still remembered the fluid beauty of her body as she danced and the silken heat of her mouth when they'd kissed.

And now, heaven help him, he couldn't resist the opportunity to see her again. "I'm very much involved," he said with heavy meaning, his hand tightening on the receiver. "I can be there in ten minutes. Think you can take that long to cite her?"

The man on the other end of the line chuckled. "Sure. But if you're planning to jump on her about speeding, I'd advise caution. She's already plenty mad about having to do the field sobriety tests."

Mark hung up and strode quickly to his bedroom for car keys, shirt and ID badge. He clipped the ID to his belt and flipped the tail of his shirt over it as he left the house, his mind preoccupied with images of Sheri. She'd probably be furious by the time he got there, but even arguing with her sounded good at the moment. He smiled grimly, recalling the passion of the kiss they'd shared the last time he'd seen her angry. The chances of that happening again were practically nil. But a man could dream, couldn't he?

SHERI HAD NEVER felt more conspicuous in her life. Shifting her stance on the ice-plant-bordered sidewalk, she tried not to glare at the two police officers who were laboriously filling out her traffic citation. All around her she could almost feel the gaze of curious eyes peering out of the tidy houses lining the street. She'd decided it had to be the most embarrassing moment of her life when an all too familiar Bronco pulled in to park behind the patrol car.

"No, it can't be." She groaned softly, knowing it was even before Mark Sampson got out and started toward her and the two officers. At that moment she would have been quite happy to have them haul her off to jail, just to avoid having to explain her latest misadventure.

Watching his slow, confident approach, she had an unwelcome memory of the latent power of his trim body and how it felt pressed hard against her own. Today there was an added element. Even dressed in bleached-out jeans and a pale yellow aviator-style shirt, he exuded an air of authority that his fellow officers also seemed to sense. They greeted him deferentially as he casually revealed the ID badge clipped to his belt. And after Mark had assured them he would handle the situation from that point, they quickly handed Sheri her copy of the traffic citation and retreated to their car.

As they drove off, Mark turned to Sheri, who had maintained a tight-lipped silence throughout the exchange. "Aren't you even going to say hello?"

She groaned and buried her face in her hands for a moment. "I'm sorry. I never dreamed they'd actually ask you to come down here." Then, gesturing in frustration at the disappearing patrol car, she added with renewed heat, "It's bad enough that they gave me a speeding ticket, considering I'm the victim in all this."

"Victim?" Mark folded his arms across his chest and gave her a measuring look. "Have you stopped to consider what might have happened if a small child had run out into the street while you were playing cops and robbers?"

Sheri's anger whooshed out of her like air escaping a punctured tire as she realized the possible consequences of her pursuit. She bit her lip and looked away from Mark's steady gaze. "You're right, of course. I just didn't think...." She threw her hands out in a gesture of surrender. "All right, go ahead and say it. I'm irresponsible, thoughtless, selfish—"

"Quit putting words in my mouth," Mark interrupted, capturing her hands to still their wild movement. "I'm not condemning you for that. In fact, I might have done same thing." At Sheri's skeptical look he added, "Even I give in to impulses occasionally."

"I find that hard to imagine." She lowered her gaze to her hands, which were pressed together inside his much larger grasp. His words had brought a surprising sense of exoneration, and with it the unsettling realization that she cared a great deal about his opinion of her.

"I kissed you, didn't I?"

His words sent sensual echoes rippling through her body, and she felt a glowing warmth spread along her cheekbones as she looked up at him. She'd tried to avoid thinking about that kiss for the past three weeks, but now the memory blazed in her mind like a neon sign. Tugging her hands from his grip, she muttered uneasily, "I thought we'd agreed to forget that."

"Maybe, but I haven't been able to do it. Why do you think I rushed down here when that beat cop called?"

His directness made her even more wary. "I don't know... maybe to gloat?"

Mark's jawline flexed visibly as he clenched his teeth. "There you go, misinterpreting my motives again."

Sheri combed her fingers through the heavy bangs that dipped over her forehead. "As you may recall, that's one of the things I seem to do best." She gestured helplessly and frowned when she saw that she still held the traffic citation. "This is just great," she grumbled, stuffing the offensive paper into her purse. "A ticket right on the tail of having my car stolen. My insurance company will probably cancel me."

"That doesn't necessarily follow. You can go to traffic school, and the ticket will never appear on your record. If you like, I can get you a list of the ones available around town."

Relief washed through her in a gentle stream, and she rewarded him with a smile. "I forgot about the school option. Thanks for reminding me." She gazed at him for a moment, captivated by the warm regard she saw in his eyes. Awareness bloomed between them, as it had during their last telephone conversation, and this time she couldn't brush it off with humor. Not with him looking at her that way.

Finally Mark broke the awkward silence. "Are you . . . ? That is . . . I was wondering if you have a little free time this afternoon. There's something I'd like to show you."

From habit she hesitated. "I don't know. I should get back to my store." Except that she didn't really have to, not with Sean in charge.

Mark's gaze swept down and away. He seemed to have accepted her refusal so abruptly that it prompted her to ask, "What do you want me to see?"

He shrugged and hooked his thumbs under his belt. "We raided a chop shop the other day, and I thought you might like to see what kind of odds I'm up against when it comes to recovering a stolen car."

"What in the world is a chop shop?"

He looked up again and gave her his stunning grin. "It's slang for a place where stolen vehicles are cut up and sold as used parts. This is one of the biggest we've ever found." He shrugged again. "You might find it interesting."

Caught by the magic of his smile and intrigued beyond any further hesitation, Sheri accepted. They set off in his Bronco, stopping only long enough for her to call Sean and say she would be gone a while longer.

As they headed south on the freeway, a shimmering excitement began to fill the interior of the vehicle. At first Sheri assumed she alone could feel it, because Mark began to give her a short course on the finer points of an auto-theft ring. But then she noticed his fingertips drumming an agitated rhythm against the steering wheel, and as the tension mounted, his comments and her responses grew more and more stilted. By the time he pulled up in front of an abandoned poultry ranch on the outskirts of National City, just south of San Diego, they were barely speaking.

"This is it?" Sheri inquired, glad to have something to say. She hadn't felt this tongue-tied since junior high school. "I expected it to look more like an auto-repair shop."

Mark shook his head. "This guy didn't concern himself with fixing cars—just wrecking them. Come on, I'll show you around." He got out, and Sheri quickly followed suit.

The place appeared deserted, the only sign of life coming from a breeze that stirred the tall weeds growing among the collection of ramshackle buildings. And cars—she couldn't begin to guess how many—in various stages of destruction. Everywhere she looked, their rusting hulks bulged out of the open-sided buildings and rested in untidy rows. The sight depressed her more than she would have believed possible. Each of those cars represented someone like herself—an innocent victim unfairly deprived of his or her property.

"Watch your step," Mark instructed quietly, taking her hand as they started toward the nearest building. "The ground isn't too even here, and there are rusty nails and stuff scattered all over."

Sheri nodded, wondering at the immense comfort she experienced at the touch of his hand. When she peered into a dirt-filmed window of the structure, however, her mood darkened. Inside was an assortment of sports cars, including a Mercedes 450SL nearly identical to hers. It had been sawn in half.

Appalled, she took a quick step back. "That could have been my car."

"Yours might end up like that yet," Mark observed, turning from the window to look at her. "Especially if the guy you saw driving it today thinks you can ID him. That car can be used as evidence against him, especially if the vehicle identification number on the dash is still intact. Sometimes they pry it off, but even that isn't enough, because the number is repeated on various hidden parts of the vehicle. If this guy's smart, he'll chop the car for parts as soon as possible."

"Gee, thanks," Sheri snapped, blinking against a sudden burning sensation in her eyes. Not tears, she told herself stubbornly. "I can't tell you how much better that makes me feel." The burning intensified, and to save face she turned and ran toward the Bronco.

She'd only managed to give the handle of the locked door one yank when Mark caught up with her and reached around to unlock it. Silently he opened the door and allowed her to get in, saying only, "Sheri, I'm sorry," before he closed it.

When he got in on his side she kept her face averted, waiting for the sound of the engine. Instead Mark's voice reached out like a stroking hand. "Tell me about him."

She didn't turn around. "Who?"

"Your father. You told me he gave you the car just before he died. If losing it upsets you this much, I can imagine how you felt about him. I'd like to know what kind of man he was."

She looked around in surprise and discovered he meant it. Using one hand to squeeze the nape of her neck, she laughed softly and answered, "Not what you'd expect. In fact, most people thought he was a feckless scoundrel. He turned his back on the wealth and prestige of his family's business. As far as I know, he never held a steady job. He never got around to marrying my mother, and he left when Sean and I were toddlers."

"Doesn't exactly sound like hero material." Mark reached to cup her chin. "So why did you love the guy so much?" His blue eyes reflected nothing more than an honest need to know, compelling her to answer with equal honesty.

"Because I knew he loved us. He always kept in touch with Sean and me, regardless of what part of the world he was in. Even sent a little money when he had it." She paused, tightening her lips into a grimace. "And because I knew exactly why he'd turned out the way he had the day I had my first encounter with his mother. My grandmother liked to control things."

"Sounds like she may have tried to control you."

Sheri gave him a wry smile. "How did you guess? She took Sean and me away from our mother when we were twelve. The court battle was ugly, to say the least. Grandmother claimed she wanted to provide us with respectability. She even made us take our father's name. But she never let us forget that we weren't legitimate." She pulled back and gave him a challenging look. "Does my being a bastard shock you?"

Mark shook his head slowly. "Not at all." He hesitated and glanced out the windshield. "My daughter April was almost illegitimate. Fortunately I found out she was on the way and talked her mother into marrying me instead of going through an adoption or having an abortion. The marriage was a mistake, but I've never regretted having April."

"Tina says she's a great kid."

He looked back at her and the intensity of his gaze caused a little flutter-thump in her chest. "You two talked about me? What else did Tina say?"

Sheri hesitated. She couldn't tell him they'd discussed the very personal topic of his disastrous marriage. He'd probably perceive it as an invasion of his privacy. So she dodged the issue by changing the subject. "Why are we having this conversation? I thought we agreed we didn't suit each other."

Mark leaned closer and the last rays of the afternoon sun silvered his hair with platinum. "I may have said that, but it hasn't stopped me from thinking about you or from wanting to know more. Tell me, Sheri."

The urgency of his request ran through her like a current, overriding resistance, enticing compliance.

"What do you want to know?" she asked warily.

"Anything you're willing to tell me."

She closed her eyes and gave in to the seductive yearning in his voice. "All right. Where shall I start?"

"Your childhood. Tell me what it was like growing up in a circus."

Eyes still closed, she leaned her head back against the seat and smiled. "Mostly it was wonderful. The travel, the excitement of the shows, the sense of camaraderie...." Her smile widened. "Not having to go to a regular school all the time. But there were bad times, too. Like when we didn't have enough bookings to fill the season, or when the gate wasn't good. We were a small operation compared to the big names like Barnum and Bailey, and everyone had a variety of jobs to do. Overall it was the happiest time of my life."

"What about your mother? Couldn't she do anything to keep your grandmother from taking you away?"

Sheri sighed. "She tried, but she had too many strikes against her. For one, Sean and I weren't getting a proper education. For another, there were some...uh, discipline problems."

"Does that mean she let you and your brother run wild?"

She opened her eyes and found Mark leaning toward her, his expression concerned. "You have to understand," she explained with another sigh. "My mother never was the maternal type. Oh, she loved us in her way, but the day-to-day process of child rearing wasn't her strong point. She knew that better than anyone else. I think she actually let Grandmother win the custody fight, especially after she found out about me and Carlo."

Mark's eyebrows shot up. "Carlo? Who's he?"

He looked so suspicious, she couldn't resist teasing. "Carlo performed on the trapeze, among other things. He was nineteen, and at twelve I thought he was terribly mature. My mother caught us...um, experimenting."

"Experimenting—how?" He leaned even closer, and she could see much more than suspicion in his eyes. A swirling mix of jealousy and desire lurked in those clear blue depths.

She took a slow breath, knowing precisely where they were headed, but too caught up in the moment to stop it. "Carlo taught me how to kiss."

"And he did a damn fine job," Mark muttered, closing the remaining distance between them.

She closed her eyes and felt the warm, moist brush of his tongue on her lips. "Mark..." she whispered. He captured the sound with his first kiss, a slow and unrelenting seduction of her mouth.

"Did he kiss you like that?" he inquired, when lack of air forced them to pause.

"No, not nearly that much finesse. Carlo tended to be a little . . . primitive." This time Mark's possession of her mouth was swift and uncompromising, his tongue demanding. She felt his strong hands gripping her head, angling her mouth to ease his way to ever deeper exploration. The power of it stunned her, and when he broke away they were both gasping.

"If you were trying to prove a point, consider it done," she said unsteadily.

Mark groaned and pushed himself back into the driver's seat, then braced his arms on the steering wheel. "I shouldn't have done that. Talk to me, Sheri."

She stared at him, perplexed. "About what?"

"Something . . . anything to get my mind off what I want to do right now." *Like tossing you into that back seat and discovering if I'm still capable of the feats I managed when I was a teenager.*

Sheri tried to stifle a giggle and got a scowl for her efforts.

"It isn't funny."

"Yes, it is." She grinned. "You'd probably injure yourself in that back seat."

Mark's frown deepened. "How did you know I was thinking about the back seat?"

Sheri groaned silently. She'd read his thoughts again, and this time it had seemed so natural, she'd forgotten it wasn't part of their audible conversation. "Well . . ." she stalled, thinking fast. "I was a teenager too, you know."

"Teenager? How did . . . ?"

"I mean, almost anyone who'd been a teenager would be thinking about back seats after a kiss like that." *Pretty weak,* she told herself. *Time for a change of topic.* "Let me tell you about my grandmother. With a single glance she could freeze the libido of any oversexed nineteen-year-old male."

"Sounds like a real sweetheart. You talk. I'll drive." Mark put the key into the ignition and started the engine, then sent her a telling look. "And don't think I didn't catch that clever allusion to the state of my libido."

Sheri laughed and proceeded to give him a highly edited version of life under the thumb of Marcelline O'Reilly. To her surprise, he managed to read a lot between the lines.

"From what you say, you and your brother must have been a handful, but your grandmother reminds me of a drill instructor I had in the marines. No wonder you rebelled, especially when she sent your brother away to school."

They were cruising down Interstate 5 toward the Kensington district, where she'd left her brother's car. Sheri fixed her attention on the surrounding traffic and said quietly, "That was the hardest part. Sean and I had been very...close up until then, but it never was the same after she separated us. Sean changed somehow. Education became the single most important thing in his world." She turned to give Mark an earnest look. "He's really quite bright, in spite of what you might think of his current occupation. He collected degrees like some people collect stamps. He could have his pick of any number of careers."

"Are you saying he became a mime to rebel against your grandmother?"

"Not exactly. He didn't really start that until after she'd died. But he did show every sign of becoming a professional student for a long time. And she didn't live long enough to see him put any of his education to use."

Mark stroked his chin thoughtfully. "So what did you do to rebel?"

"Nothing too outrageous beyond the belly dancing." She sent him a wry look. "Believe it or not, I actually tried to please her for a while. Don't ask me why. I think she just wore me down. I even went so far as to marry a man she thought was—" She stopped, distressed at what she'd just revealed. For that matter, she'd done practically all of the revealing in their conversation. How had that happened?

"Wrong guy, huh?" Mark's voice sounded gruff.

She nodded stiffly, and they rode in uncomfortable silence until he pulled in and parked behind Sean's white Volkswagen. Outside, the street lamps had begun to glow in the first encroachment of twilight. When he turned toward her, one hand coming to rest on the back of her seat, she quickly grabbed her purse and prepared to get out.

"Sheri, wait."

She opened the door and hopped outside before responding. "I'd better hurry. Sean's going to wonder what happened to me. Thanks for an . . . interesting afternoon." She closed the door before he could reply, but he caught up with her as she fumbled with the VW's lock.

"You can't just go waltzing off like this." His hand pushed against the car's door, holding it shut. In the deepening twilight his face looked grim. "Why are you so upset all of a sudden? Was it that reference to your ex?"

With a sigh of resignation, she faced him. "What do you want from me, Mark Sampson? You spent the afternoon pumping me for my life story, yet I know practically nothing about you. You kiss me like there's no tomorrow, but we both know there is. And for me tomorrow means looking beyond the first rush of desire. Are you any closer to accepting me as I am—belly dancing and all?"

Mark hesitated, and when he spoke again, Sheri had to give him credit for his honesty. "I don't know, but this afternoon made me realize I'd like to find out." He teased her with a grin. "And it wasn't just the kissing."

She folded her arms across her chest. "Okay, what are you suggesting?"

"We could start with dinner. Maybe some seafood—tonight?"

"I adore seafood, but I'm busy tonight and tomorrow night."

"Monday night, then. I know a great place right on the beach."

She cocked her head to one side and considered. "All right, but there won't be any kissing. I don't find it conducive to making levelheaded decisions."

Mark chuckled and opened the car door for her. "How about heavy breathing? Am I allowed that?" He snapped his fingers. "Which reminds me, whatever happened to your anonymous caller?"

"I think he finally gave up on me." She slid into the driver's seat and looked up at him. "He hasn't bothered me since the night you called."

"I can understand why, after the way you answered my call." He laughed when she made a face at him. "What time shall I pick you up on Monday?"

"You'd better make it early. Say five-thirty?"

He nodded, started to close the door, then leaned down and into the car. His voice took on a sexy drawl as he said, "I'll be looking forward to it, even if there isn't going to be any kissing."

Sheri rolled her eyes and started the car. But as she drove off, the sensual aftermath of his words warmed her until she was forced to lower the driver's side window for a cooling breeze.

SUNDAY NIGHT'S jazz session always put Sheri into a jubilant mood, and she hummed along with the music as she prepared cups of espresso and served pastries. She paused in midnote when one of her part-time girls approached, looking distressed.

"What's up, Annie? You look upset."

"It's that huge guy in the denim jacket who's been lurking around the doorway. He gives me the creeps."

Sheri's gaze automatically went to the door. "I don't see anyone there now. He probably just stopped for a minute to listen to the music."

"It looked to me like he was more interested in watching you."

A flicker of unease tickled the back of her mind, but she squelched it with a laugh. "A secret admirer? How flattering!"

"Seriously, Sheri, I didn't like the looks of the guy."

"All right, if it'll make you feel better, I'll have Sean go check it out."

Sean returned after a thorough look around and said he hadn't seen anyone fitting Annie's description. For Sheri that was the end of it, although she did make sure Sean walked Annie to her car after they'd closed for the evening.

When Sheri dropped Sean at his apartment, she once again brought up the subject of getting herself a loaner car. "I can't keep using your car all the time," she protested. "And the insurance company said they'd reimburse me until they decide to declare the Mercedes a write-off."

Sean stopped trying to get his long legs out of the car long enough to chasten her with a frown. "I told you before, I prefer riding my bike. So I rarely need the car during the day. Why not save the insurance company a little money? They might be more willing to renew your policy."

"Well, if you're sure . . ."

"I'm sure." He hesitated, his dark eyes searching hers. "There's something I'd like to ask you. If I'm overstepping, just say so."

Sheri braced herself; he sounded serious. "Okay, shoot."

"What's going on with you and this Mark Sampson guy? You told me once you were experiencing thought transference with him. But you also said there wasn't any chance of you two getting together. Then the other day you disappeared for the whole afternoon with him, and when you got back you looked . . . I don't know . . . different."

"That obvious, huh?" She grinned ruefully. "The truth is I don't know what's going on yet. I'm having dinner with him tomorrow night to see if we can work something out."

"I'd like to see that happen for you, with the right guy." He swiveled his gaze to look out the windshield. "I remember how it was when we were kids, the sharing, the closeness." He laughed softly. "Remember that mind-reading act we did? No one, not even our own mother suspected we didn't need secret signals to pass information—that we simply read each other's thoughts. Sometimes I wish I hadn't ended it."

Sheri reached to touch his shoulder. "It wasn't your fault. Being separated—"

"No," he interrupted harshly. "I think it's time you knew I did that purposely." He faced her, unexpected anguish in his eyes. "At first, right after Grandmother separated us, I could feel your pain as acutely as my own. Leaving the circus, making the break with Lila, I could handle that, considering she never really encouraged a close mother-son relationship. But losing you and knowing how unhappy you were with Grandmother—knowing each time she hurt you . . ." His voice cracked, and he cleared his throat uneasily. "After a while I couldn't take it anymore, so I made myself stop feeling."

"I often wondered . . ." She blinked rapidly and shook her head. "But that was years ago, and it wasn't really your fault. I made a few bad choices myself as a result of Grandmother's interference."

"Including your marriage to that stuffed shirt, Everett Masters. That's why I hoped this mind thing with Sampson might mean something. I think it's pretty obvious that you and I will never communicate like that again."

"Hey!" She gave him a soft punch on the shoulder. "It's enough just having you living nearby. I'm not pining away for deep emotional communication."

Sean eyed her doubtfully. "Or maybe you just don't realize it yet." He hauled himself out of the car, then bent to peer back at her. "Think about it. Especially tomorrow night." With that cryptic piece of advice, he slammed the door and jogged toward his apartment.

5

NERVOUSLY Sheri ran a hand over her hair and hurried to answer the knock at her front door. Ever since the night before she hadn't been able to stop thinking about Sean's advice. *Was* she secretly pining for a deep emotional commitment? And if so, how did Mark Sampson fit into the scheme?

She took a fortifying breath as she opened the door, but it didn't help. Mark smiled and she felt a rolling little jolt in her midsection. She attempted a calm smile in return, telling herself it was nothing more than sexual attraction—a simple reaction to his virile good looks. And he did look exceptionally virile, she admitted silently. His brown corduroy slacks and beige turtleneck sweater were the perfect complement to his lanky, tightly muscled body.

"Hi." Mark's voice sounded unusually gravelly, and his gaze swept over her twice in quick succession.

Nonplussed, Sheri touched the pointed collar of her fuchsia jumpsuit. "Is this all right? You said the restaurant was casual."

Mark cleared his throat. "It's...fine. Are you ready to go?"

Sheri nodded and gathered her purse and a fuchsia-and-yellow-patterned shawl from the hall table.

Fine? She'd spent an hour and a half selecting this outfit, and all he could say was "fine"? She closed and locked the door behind her with a bit more force than was necessary, then started past him toward the Bronco.

"Wait a minute." Mark's hands encircled her waist and pulled her back around to face him. "I don't think I said that right." He gave her waist a little squeeze. "You look sensational. In fact, I'm already regretting that no-kissing agreement we have."

A quick thrill shimmered through her, but she hid it behind a chastening look. "See that you don't forget it."

Forget it? Mark repeated to himself as he followed her down the walkway. That was a laugh! Did she have any idea of how sexy she looked? The way that hot-pink material hugged her bottom made it hard for him to remember how hungry he'd been a few minutes ago—for food, that is.

THE RESTAURANT Mark had chosen was known for its spectacular view and for the freshness and quality of its seafood. The maître d' showed them to a table with an unobstructed view of the ocean, produced leather-bound menus and slipped quietly away. Mark gave the extensive wine list a cursory check, then set it aside to watch Sheri.

"This is beautiful!" she exclaimed, her gaze fixed on the twilight panorama outside. Sunset was only a pink-tinged memory on the horizon, and white-crowned breakers stroked the shoreline like a lover's hand.

"So are you," Mark retorted, enjoying the slightly flustered smile he got in response. A waiter appeared, and after a brief consultation with Sheri, Mark ordered a bottle of white zinfandel.

"I think we're off to a pretty good start," he announced with satisfaction when they were alone again. Sheri gave him an inquiring look that prompted him to add, "We might disagree in some areas, but we didn't have any difficulty agreeing on the wine."

Sheri gave him a dangerous little smile. "Just wait till we order dinner." She leaned toward him, her arms resting on the peach linen tablecloth. "In the meantime, why don't you tell me about yourself? I think it's only fair after the way I bared my soul the other day."

Her request caused a small reactive tightening in his gut. Talking about himself had never been easy, but the way she looked right then, the candle on their table illuminating the avid interest in her dark eyes, prompted him to try.

"My story isn't nearly as . . . exciting as yours," he began. "I was born in Fargo, North Dakota, thirty-seven years ago. I have a father, mother and two younger brothers, all of whom live in Los Angeles County now." He shrugged. "I began my career with the police department up there, but I moved here when a better job opportunity opened up." An uncomfortable memory stirred deep in his heart. He'd met Melanie in those early days in San Diego, when he'd still been new in town and lonely. Her reckless joie de vivre had temporarily filled the emptiness in him, but the price had been high . . . too high.

The waiter arrived with their wine and Mark used the time to study the lovely woman opposite him. Was history repeating itself? True, Sheri didn't seem at all self-centered, as Melanie had turned out to be, but there was a nagging familiarity in the quixotic way Sheri pursued the things she wanted. Melanie had been like that about her dancing career. The similarity gave him pause. Was he making the same mistake? Better not give away too much of himself until he found out.

Mark took a sip of the wine and purposely changed the course of the conversation. "There's something I've been wondering about since we talked the other day. You mentioned that your father died. What happened to your mother?"

"She's living in Florida with some of her old circus cronies." Sheri chuckled. "They even perform together occasionally for benefits, although Mother complains she's not as limber as she used to be."

"And what about your father? Did you get to spend any time with him before he died?"

Sheri nodded and dropped her gaze to the pale pink liquid in her wineglass. "Too little time. He came back to San Diego to stay when Grandmother willed him the bulk of her estate. He said he was ready to settle down at last." Sheri looked up, and he saw a deep sadness in her eyes. "It never occurred to me he'd come home to die. We only had a short time together." She frowned suddenly. "How did we get on the subject of me again?"

He grinned and toasted her with his glass. "I think you're more interesting. How did you get started selling coffee?"

"I got the idea when I was in Paris, learning to make pastries." She tasted her wine, drawing his attention to the moist, sweet curve of her mouth.

After a moment he managed, "Why didn't you ever go back to the circus?"

"I did for a short time after I graduated from high school." She shook her head sadly. "It wasn't the same. Too many sad memories, I guess. I finally gave up and went to college."

"So why pastries in Paris?"

She gave him a wry glance. "Isn't that what everyone does after a nasty divorce?"

Mark didn't have an answer for that. He was too busy fighting the hot flash of resentment that burned in his gut at the thought of another man having her and hurting her. Which was totally unfair, considering his earlier reservations about getting involved with her himself.

The waiter returned to take their order, and when he glanced at Sheri she announced, "I'll have a garden salad." A challenge sparkled in her eyes. "And the fresh oysters on the half shell."

Mark tried to look nonchalant. "Raw oysters?" he inquired tentatively.

"Of course." Her eyes rounded in mock dismay. "You wouldn't expect me to eat them cooked, would you?"

He realized a gauntlet had been thrown and quickly shook his head. "Never. Would you like anything else?" When she declined with a smile, he placed his own more conservative order for a grilled swordfish steak and baked potato.

When he turned back to Sheri, he found her biting her lip to keep from laughing. "Is it going to bother you, watching me eat raw oysters?" she asked after a moment. "If it is, I can change my order to something more conventional."

"I can take it if you can," he declared staunchly, then frowned when her laughter bubbled out. "What's so funny?"

"I was just remembering the last time I ordered them on a date. The poor guy turned pea green and had to leave the table." She giggled. "Funny, I never heard from him again."

Suddenly, unexpectedly, Mark felt swamped with delight. Her irrepressible nature charmed him, even when she was deliberately baiting him. He relaxed and settled back into his chair. "You won't get rid of me that easily," he said, giving her a superior smile.

The evening seemed to take an upward swing from there. As they ate, she began to tell him about the joys and trials of running her café, entertaining him with descriptions of her most colorful customers. And that led Mark to relate some of the amusing stories of his time as a beat cop.

"Did you really throw a whole pizza at him?" Sheri exclaimed, smothering her laughter with her napkin.

"Hey, it was the only weapon I had at the moment. And there was an armed robbery in progress. The owner of the pizza joint was so grateful he gave me an extra large with everything for a replacement. Taught me a lesson, though." He grinned. "Now I have my pizza delivered instead of picking it up." With a casual movement, he poured the last few drops of wine into her glass.

"I don't really need any more," she protested.

"You're forgetting, I'm driving." *Besides, you might be more inclined to forget your rule about kissing if you drink it,* he added silently. *And after watching that sexy mouth of yours all evening, I'm desperate enough to try anything.*

He heard her take a quick breath and saw an odd darkening in her eyes, almost as if she knew what he'd been thinking. Of course, she probably did; it didn't take a genius to figure out the old "ply 'em with wine" move. Chagrined at his own transparency, he tried to make amends.

"You don't have to drink it. If you're finished we can go now, maybe take a stroll on the beach."

She nodded and bent to pick up her purse. "Actually, I think you'd better take me home. I have to be up at the crack of dawn, or there'll be a lot of grumpy people going to work without their morning coffee."

Mark saw through her half-hearted attempt at humor and felt even worse. *She probably thinks you have a one-track mind,* he told himself as he followed her outside. The problem was, at that moment he did.

FOR SHERI, the ride back to her home seemed to escalate the tension that had hummed just below the surface of their conversation all evening. Sexual tension—there was no other way to describe it. She would have sensed it even if she hadn't known his exact thought when he gave her the last of the wine. They'd continued to talk, but the topics had been inconsequential, the kind people used to fill awkward silences.

By the time she'd unlocked her door and pushed it open a crack, her nerves were stretched taut between the cautioning voice of experience and the sultry call of desire. She started to say good-night without turning around, but his hand on her shoulder brought her about until she felt the doorjamb pressing against her spine.

"You're upset with me," he stated quietly.

She lowered her eyes and shook her head in silent denial.

"Then look at me, and tell me why I feel as if you've been pushing away from me since we left the restaurant."

She raised her eyes, and the raw vulnerability in his features caused her heart to pound in double time. "I'm not upset with you," she murmured. "I'm just..."

She considered for a moment, then opted for honesty. "I'm a little wary of the effect we seem to have on each other. I know we agreed there would be no kissing, but I'm not too sure I'd be able to hold you to it if you decided to renege." She bit her lip and frowned. "*That* upsets me."

Mark's mouth began to tilt in to a slow, sensual smile. "Why? What's wrong with giving in to what we both want?"

When her gaze shifted to the partially open door and the long, dimly lit hallway beyond, understanding warmed his eyes. "I get it. We're not restricted by location this time, are we? If you let me kiss you and we got carried away, all I'd have to do is sweep you up in my arms and head down that hall until I found the bedroom."

"You have to admit, we did get rather carried away the last time." Just thinking about it made her feel hot and shivery inside, but that didn't solve anything. "And I'm still not sure if I'm ready for . . . that."

"You know, the first time I saw you I would have been surprised to hear what you just said." Slowly he brought one hand up to frame the side of her face. "Now it sounds perfectly natural."

She gasped a little as the tough, yet smooth pad of his thumb glided across her lower lip, then repeated the caress, following the curving line of the upper. Again he stroked and again, his touch light and soft, sensitizing her mouth until it quivered. "Wh-what about our agreement?" she managed in an airy voice.

"I'm not kissing you." The color of his eyes deepened to a smoky blue. "I just want to see if you're as hungry for it as I am."

In answer she caught his thumb between her teeth and gently bit down. His breath hissed in and his fingers plowed into the depths of her hair, tipping her head back as he brought his mouth to within an inch of hers. "Next time, no agreements," he whispered, his breath gusting warm against her lips. He released her and gently propelled her toward the doorway. "Now get inside and lock the door before I lose my resolve."

IN THE MIDST of a lingering sensual haze, Sheri moved through her nightly bedtime ritual. As she brushed her teeth, she could still feel the seductive stroking of Mark's thumb on her lips, and had to admit she half regretted his fortitude. How easy it would have been if he'd lost control and taken the decision out of her hands!

She made a face at herself in the bathroom mirror. Now she sounded like one of those weak-kneed Victorian maidens who were constantly being swept away by the animal passions of some male. But as she touched her fingertips to her mouth, his words resounded again and again in her mind. *Next time . . . Next time . . .*

The telephone rang and her first thought was *Mark!* She rushed to answer it in the kitchen, her red satin robe swirling around her ankles. But his voice didn't respond to her breathless hello. There was only heavy silence.

Irritated, Sheri snapped, "Listen, stupid, I thought we were finished with this. Find someone else to bother."

She started to hang up, but stopped when a low, thick voice said, "Don't . . . don't hang up on me like the other times, Sheri. I got information on your car. You want it back?"

Sheri's pulse began to pound. This wasn't just an annoyance call anymore. The man had used her name and knew about her car. Mark must have been right; the calls had been related to the theft. "Who is this?"

The sound of a long, indrawn breath came over the line. "A friend. That's all I wanta be. I thought we could meet somewhere and . . . uh, talk about your car. Unless you don't want it no more."

"I want it," she said without hesitation. But her hands began to shake so hard, she had to grip the receiver with both of them. "Tell me how much."

"Not yet. First you have to prove to me you won't call the cops. I don't like cops."

"I won't." Lying didn't count in a situation like this, did it?

"Prove it. Meet me tomorrow night, eight o'clock, at the Blue Fox Tavern." He droned out an address in Chula Vista, a city about fifteen miles south of San Diego. "And come alone. If you don't, I'll know and the deal's off." The line went dead before she could respond.

She stood there for a moment, shivering in reaction. She'd just spoken to a criminal—and agreed to meet him. Now what?

The obvious answer came to her immediately. With trembling hands she pulled Mark's business card from the little bulletin board hanging next to the phone and dialed the home number he'd scrawled onto the back. As she listened to the ringing at the other end of the line, she closed her eyes and tried to organize her thoughts. He wasn't going to like this latest development, of that she was certain.

The sound of his husky "Hello?" reached out to encircle her like a comforting hug.

"Mark, it's Sheri. I . . . I hope I didn't wake you."

His voice deepened even more. "No. I was just lying here thinking about you and telling myself how much I hate being honorable. If you've changed your mind, don't tell me. I already sent April's sitter home."

"No, it's not that. I had another of those calls just now, except . . . he talked to me, used my name."

"When?" Mark demanded, instantly all business. "Tell me exactly what he said."

Sheri took a deep breath and began a short recap of the conversation.

"Absolutely not!" he interrupted, the minute she got to the part about a meeting at the Blue Fox. "Do you have any idea what kind of dive that place probably is? I can tell just by the address."

"I wasn't planning on going alone. I thought you might be interested in catching this guy."

"I am, but I doubt he'll have the car with him, and I can't arrest him without probable cause. If you want my opinion, I don't think he has any intention of returning that car at any price. The whole thing could be a setup."

Sheri swallowed nervously. "For what purpose?"

"I don't know. Maybe it's you he's interested in." Mark swore softly. "I had a hunch those breather calls were connected when they came right on the tail of the car theft. But when you said they'd stopped and there didn't appear to be any other signs, I let it drop."

A chilling little memory crystallized in her mind. "Maybe there was something," she began uneasily. "Sunday night during the jazz concert, one of my employees claimed there was a big creepy guy watching me from the doorway of the shop. I didn't think anything of it, especially after Sean checked outside and didn't find anything suspicious. But now I can't help but wonder. . . ." She cut herself off with a disgusted little laugh. "This is starting to sound like one of those cheap horror shows. Next you'll have me looking askance at every customer who comes through my door."

"I didn't intend that. Although there've been some pretty weird characters hanging around the area whenever I've stopped by. I just want you to understand why I don't want you to go to that bar. The fact that this guy has gone from merely breathing at you to asking you to meet him tells me he could be after more than a little conversation. On the other hand, if you don't show up he might get discouraged and never bother you again."

Her jaw tightened in resolution. "I refuse to sit around like a coward and wait for some lowlife to harass me. And if there's a chance I might get my car back in the process of catching the culprit, I'm willing to risk it. If you're not interested in helping me, I'll ask someone else, like Lou."

Mark groaned. "You know I can't let you do that. And I'm not suggesting cowardice, just caution. In case you haven't noticed, I've developed a personal interest in your safety."

Again that warm comforting sensation engulfed her, and she absently brought one end of her robe's satin sash to her lips and rubbed it back and forth. "Was there a yes buried somewhere in that last declaration?" she asked, her mouth beginning to curve in a smile.

Mark's sigh sounded like a roaring wind in her ear. "Only if you agree that I'm in charge. I have had a little more experience in dealing with this sort of situation."

"Whatever you say, boss," she said, glad he couldn't see her grin of relief. "What should I do first?"

"*You* don't do anything. I'm going to check out the Blue Fox tomorrow, during the day. Then I'll tell you what the plan is. For now I'd suggest you try to get some rest. Who knows what tomorrow night will bring?"

"All right. Good night, Mark." She started to hang up, but his voice came again.

"Will you feel uneasy being alone tonight?"

"I'll be fine," she assured him quickly. "After all, he's called before and nothing happened."

"I'd offer to come over, but like I said, the sitter went home."

"It's probably just as well," she said, then drew the slippery red satin over her lips one more time before adding, "I might talk you out of being honorable. Sweet dreams, Mark." She heard his frustrated moan as she hung up.

"Okay, one more time. Tell me what you're supposed to do." Mark's voice sounded strained in the quiet darkness of the Bronco's interior. They had driven it at his insistence to Chula Vista's nightlife district, and were now parked on a side street three blocks away from the Blue Fox.

Sheri reined in her impatience and repeated for the third time, "I park on the street in front of the place. I go inside, sit in the last booth and wait. If anybody approaches me, I try to find out if he's the guy who called. If he isn't, I get rid of him. If he is, I signal you by knocking my purse on the floor. Above all else, I'm not to give any sign of encouragement to any male in the place."

"Lord knows, the way you look will accomplish that," Mark muttered.

"What's wrong with this outfit?" Sheri demanded, looking down at her black jeans with their matching jacket. Under the jacket she wore a red turtleneck sweater. "I thought you told me to dress unobtrusively."

"I would have preferred something that didn't fit quite so well." He shifted in his seat and pulled a large, nasty-looking gun from his leather jacket.

Sheri had been ready to comment on the hip-hugging fit of his Levi's, but the words died on her lips. She watched with growing horror as he spun the cylinder to check the load. "Good heavens! What do you intend to do with that?"

He smiled grimly and replaced the weapon in its holster. "Nothing, I hope. Like I told you, the most I can do in a setup like this is ID the guy and lean on him a little. I can't arrest him for talking to you, much as the idea appeals to me. At the most I can tell him to leave you alone. If we're incredibly lucky, he might be intimidated enough or dumb enough to tell us something about the car. But I wouldn't count on it, if I were you."

Without warning her stubborn show of bravado slipped, and she had to clasp her hands together tightly to hide their trembling. "Uh...I suppose there's no reason to be nervous, right?"

"That's what you keep telling me," he replied dryly. But when he glanced her way, his expression softened, and he covered her cold hands with his large warm ones. "Hey, you can still back out, if you want."

And admit defeat to some cheap creep who thought he could steal her car and harass her at will? She shook her head so vehemently that her long hair, confined in a black clip, swished against her back. "No. I want to do it." She brushed futilely at several tendrils that had escaped to curl around her ears.

Mark intercepted her hand and brought it to his lips for a brief, reassuring kiss. His mouth felt warm and firm against her fingertips. "Then stop worrying. As you've said at least a hundred times, 'What can happen in a public place?'"

A PUNGENT HAZE of cigarette smoke swirled around Sheri as she stepped into the dim interior of the Blue Fox. She gave the room a furtive once-over and decided Mark had been right. The place was a real dive.

Lurid beer and liquor advertisements papered the walls, most of them featuring top-heavy young women intent on displaying their charms. From one corner a decrepit jukebox poured out a mournful country and western tune, the lyrics underscored by the drone of conversation and occasional raucous laughter.

A pool table stood to the right of the door, and several men dressed in jeans, some with denim jackets, some in T-shirts, lounged around it. Three more similarly clad patrons were sitting together at the bar, each with a beer or straight shot—or both—in front of him. At the end of the bar sat a fourth man, his huge body hunched so far over his beer, it appeared as if he might be trying to drown himself.

High-backed booths lined the wall to her right, but the dim light prevented her from seeing how many of them held customers. She had an uneasy feeling there weren't any females among them.

Don't think about it, she ordered herself silently. She squared her shoulders and started toward the last booth in the back, keenly aware of the silent scrutiny of every male she passed. So much for being unobtrusive. With great relief she slipped onto the hard wooden bench that faced the front of the room. From there she could keep an eye on almost everyone, and the booth gave her a sense of security, even if it meant sitting in deeper darkness.

After a few minutes the bartender leaned over the bar and growled an inquiry about what she wanted to drink. To appease him she ordered a diet soft drink, which he delivered with a disgusting leer.

"You waitin' for someone?"

Sheri bit back a pithy response and simply said, "Yes."

"Thought so. You don't exactly fit in here."

How very astute of you, she thought, handing him several bills. He grinned, displaying cigarette-stained teeth, when she told him to keep the change. To her chagrin he propped one hand upon the table, apparently ready to chat, but she was saved when the front door swung open and Mark Sampson strolled in with the nonchalance of a regular.

For Sheri it was a stunning revelation. Here was a side of the man she'd never expected to see—a cop working under cover. He acknowledged the players at the pool table with a infinitesimal lift of his head, then swung onto a bar stool with negligent ease. Every line of his body radiated masculine self-possession.

Sheri caught herself staring and jerked her gaze to the skinny plastic straw in her drink. Good grief, she'd considered him attractive before, but the way he looked right now brought a wild surge of longing. Not an appropriate response at the moment, she reminded herself grimly.

The bartender, seeing he had a new customer to attend, sighed in annoyance and went back to his post. Mark ordered a beer, then gave the room another casual glance, his gaze unhesitating when it swept over the booth in which she sat.

To avoid looking at him, she alternated between pretending to sip her drink and swirling the ice in the glass. Minutes slogged by, and tension began to build inside her like the steam in the old calliope from her circus days. She tried humming along with the jukebox music, but the twangy yodeling soon set her teeth on edge.

More minutes passed on leaden feet. She glanced at her watch and was distressed to see she'd been there a quarter of an hour. How much longer? The guy on the phone had said eight o'clock and it was eight-fifteen now. Mark had declared they would leave at nine, whether or not there was any contact.

She drummed her fingertips on the Formica table-top, her nails clicking in countertempo to the music. "Come on, you turkey, you're late," she muttered. Maybe he couldn't tell time. He hadn't sounded overly bright on the phone.

Another fifteen minutes dragged by, then she nearly jumped out of her seat when the bartender suddenly appeared beside her, asking if she'd like another drink. She felt like screaming, "No!" but managed to restrain her response to a simple head shake.

The pool game broke up and she tensed when two of the players moved to the bar and began casting speculative glances her way. Other than a few patrons trooping past on their way to or from the rest rooms in back, no one came near her.

Another five minutes passed and she began to wonder if the whole thing had been a hoax. The idea sparked her temper. Then another thought occurred to her.

What if her mystery caller was one of the men who'd entered after she'd arrived? Would he be able to see her in the stygian depths of this booth?

She checked her watch again. Only fifteen minutes left. Maybe she should make herself more visible. But how? The door behind her booth swung open, providing inspiration. The rest room! Surely the walk to and from would prove ample time for anyone to identify her.

Trying hard to appear casual, Sheri slid out of the booth and slowly stood up. She allowed herself one look around the room before strolling toward the door labeled Rest Rooms. Beyond it she found a cramped hallway with two doors appropriately labeled in English and Spanish. Inside the dingy cubicle designated Women—*Damas*, she quickly washed her hands. Her reflection looked pale and apprehensive in the cracked mirror above the sink.

Mark had been right, she thought, shaking her hands to dry them when she discovered there weren't any paper towels. This had been a fool's errand and there wasn't any point in wasting more time on it. She'd go out to the Bronco and wait for him, as they'd agreed.

She opened the door and started out, then stopped abruptly when she saw two men waiting for her in the narrow passageway. They were of similar height and build, and each had his hair skinned back into a ponytail. Right away she recognized them as the pair from the pool table, and from the predatory slant of their smiles she surmised they now had a completely different game in mind. Was one of them the man she was supposed to meet? Why had she left the relative safety of the bar's main room?

The one on the right spoke, his thick Southern drawl eliminating him as a possibility. The caller might have been slow of speech, but he hadn't come from the South. "Hey, darlin', you look kinda lonely. Want some company?"

Her apprehension deepened, but she refused to show it. "No, thanks. I'm meeting someone."

The man on her left narrowed his eyes. "Change of plans, gorgeous. You're goin' with us." He lunged at her, clamping one hand over her mouth and the other around her upper body to immobilize her arms.

Raw panic drove Sheri to respond with every ounce of her strength, twisting and struggling against his steel-hard grip. She stomped upon his foot, and when he slackened his hold in pained surprise, she jerked around and brought her knee up hard. Her assailant wasn't as lucky as Mark had been the night she'd fought with him; this time the blow landed right on target.

A vile oath sounded in her ear, and the wounded man shoved her away as he doubled over. But her freedom was short-lived. Strong arms encircled her from behind, crushing her breasts, and a callused hand stifled her attempt to cry for help.

"You're a real hellcat, aren't you?" her new captor snarled. The yeasty stench of cheap beer assailed her nostrils. "I can't wait to see what you're like in the sack." He snickered. "After what you just did to Charlie, I may have you all to myself for a while."

Sheri stiffened and tried to resist as he began to push her down the hall toward a back exit. *Mark! Mark! Where are you?* she cried desperately, but the scream went no farther than her mind. She intensified her struggles, but the man half carrying her didn't seem fazed. They had nearly reached the door when a voice as cold and hard as tempered steel rang out from behind them.

"Take one more step with her, you bastard, and I'll blow your head off!"

6

A LONG, BREATHLESS PAUSE followed Mark's lethal directive, then Sheri heard him add in a tone no less dangerous, "Let the lady go and move away from her nice and slow. That's right."

As soon as the bruising pressure left Sheri's torso, she drew a deep, gasping breath and turned unsteadily toward the sound of Mark's voice. He stood just inside the inner doorway, both hands gripping his revolver as he aimed it at the two men. His eyes were narrowed to slits, and she'd never seen a more dangerous-looking male in her life.

"Sheri, love," he said in that same dark voice. "Would you please get yourself back here with me as quickly as possible?"

She complied on shaking legs, stopping only when she stood beside him. His intense gaze flicked to her for an instant, then went back to his prisoners. But even that brief glance made her shiver. Mark Sampson looked furious, and she knew she was partly to blame.

"Are you all right?" he asked her in a low voice.

Still trying to catch her breath, she nodded. "Y-yes. I think so."

"Do you think you could go ask the bartender to call the police?"

Sheri nodded again, but didn't move at once. "Mark," she murmured unhappily, "I want to explain—"

"We'll talk about it later," he interrupted gruffly.

The situation at the Blue Fox got more complicated with the arrival of two Chula Vista police officers. Questioning the two prisoners turned into a free-for-all of accusations, counteraccusations and denials, resulting in the arrest of Sheri's would-be kidnappers only because a routine check turned up outstanding warrants for different crimes on both of them.

Throughout the procedure, Mark remained tight-lipped and coldly professional. And his demeanor didn't alter much as he drove her home afterward. Unsaid words weighed heavily between them, but her one attempt at breaking the rigid silence was turned aside by his curt request that they delay the conversation until they reached her house. By the time he'd parked in her driveway, she felt close to exploding from the tension.

Once inside, she shrugged out of her jacket and stormed down the hall to the kitchen, leaving Mark to close and lock the front door before following. As she angrily rummaged through the meager contents of her liquor cabinet, she heard him pull out a chair and sit down at her glass-topped breakfast table.

"If you're fixing drinks, I could use a stiff Scotch," he said quietly.

"I don't stock it." She turned, holding several liqueur bottles. "But I can fix you something just as effective."

"Like what?" he inquired warily, watching her grind coffee beans and scoop them into the basket of an auto-drip coffee machine.

"A B-52." The coffee started dripping through, filling the room with its strong, comforting aroma. She turned and sighed when she saw his grimace of distrust. "Basically it's just coffee laced with several different liqueurs, but it packs enough punch to live up to the name. If you'd rather, I can give you a shot of brandy, or—" she checked the shelf "—tequila."

He considered a moment, then shook his head. "I'll take whatever you're having. After all the time I spent standing around in the cold interrogating those two thugs, I could use something hot to drink."

Just thinking about what had almost happened caused a shiver to run down her spine. To prevent him from seeing it, she folded her arms across her chest. "I told you that would be a waste of time. I knew from the minute they opened their mouths that neither one was the guy who'd called me. The voices, the accents—even the vocabulary was wrong. And I don't think they were lying when they said they didn't know anything about my car."

"Just the same, I'm glad we were able to come up with an excuse to detain them. I almost came unglued when I saw that bastard dragging you toward the door." Anger burned anew in the depths of his blue eyes. "If he'd hurt you, I don't know what I would've done."

"You looked furious enough to thrash him and me," Sheri muttered. "In fact, you still look mad enough to hit me." Determined not to let him see how much his anger upset her, she turned back to the counter and began pouring the coffee into two tall slender mugs.

She heard his chair scrape back and then he was close behind her, his hands wrapped around her upper arms, pulling her back against the warm solid width of his chest. "I wasn't furious with you, just scared half out of my mind. If either of those guys had been armed—" He broke off and made a harsh, guttural sound.

Sheri felt the force of his anguish like a blow. It had never occurred to her that there might be a deeper motive behind his disapproval of the risk she'd taken. She turned in his arms and pressed her forehead against the hollow of his shoulder. Her hands moved tentatively to his chest. "Mark, I'm sorry," she whispered. "I really didn't think there was any danger...." The words seemed to catch in her throat.

Mark's embrace tightened around her. "Don't think about it anymore. It's over and you're safe. Nothing else matters."

She let out a shuddery little sigh of agreement and felt his hands slowly begin to stroke the length of her spine. After the rough handling she'd endured earlier that evening, his touch was sheer heaven. Her back arched instinctively under the caress, and she let her hands glide up until her fingertips encountered the silky brush of hair at his nape.

A low moan of approval rumbled in Mark's throat, and what had begun as a comforting gesture took on more sensual overtones. His broad palms smoothed over her hips, pressed against the indentation of her waist, then started a slow exhilarating journey up her ribs. But when he touched the tender undersides of her breasts, her murmurs of pleasure turned into soft protest.

Instantly concerned, he backed away enough to search her face. "Was I too rough? You're so soft there."

She shook her head and urged him closer again. "I'm just a little bruised, I think. That's where he...he grabbed me."

Mark uttered a low, menacing growl. "It's a good thing I didn't know that while I had a gun on him. I can't stand the idea of any other man touching you." He took her face between his hands and lowered his head until she couldn't see anything but the intense blue of his eyes. "I want it to be me. Only me."

His mouth captured hers with a seductive possessiveness that stunned her. His tongue laid a burning claim to the curve of her lips and the smooth line of her teeth before slipping inside to thrust boldly against her tongue. She tensed a little at first, expecting force, but his hands remained gentle against her cheeks, exerting only enough pressure to lure her to deeper pleasure, a pleasure so fierce, it made her hungry for more—far more. Her body ached, but from longing, not bruises.

Clasping his hands, she slowly guided them down until they curved over her breasts. When he lifted his head to regard her with surprise, she simply said, "Touch me, Mark. I want it to be you."

His eyes darkened, and his palms gently massaged her lush softness. She would have slithered to the floor if the hard edge of the counter hadn't been there to support her back. As it was, she had to close her eyes against the sweetness of the sensation. And when his fingers slipped under the fabric of her sweater to unhook her bra, her nipples contracted and grew hard in anticipation.

The first brush of his fingertips drew a gasp from her, then she could only moan softly at the maddening beauty of his touch. Just when she felt she couldn't stand a moment more, he pulled her against him again, his labored breath hot against her ear.

"Sheri, sweetheart," he said raggedly. "Let me take the sweater off. I need to see you."

Without a second thought she nodded and lifted her arms to assist him. Cool air rushed at her fevered skin, and she opened her eyes in time to see the adoration in his gaze as he reached for her yet again.

"Perfection," he murmured, lowering his lips to taste one tight, rosy nipple. "And sweet, so sweet."

Her head lolled back as his mouth closed around her, hot and moist, drawing her deeper and deeper. Desire flowed through her in fiery waves, to center in her lower body. The heat grew until she didn't think she could bear it.

Blindly she reached for Mark, and he reacted with breathtaking perception, grasping her hips to pull her tightly to him. The swollen shaft of his manhood burned against her even through the thick denim of their jeans. Mark groaned like a man in pain when she slowly rotated against him and he wrapped his arms around her to hold her still.

"Before you do any more of that, you'd better decide how far you intend to go with this," he gasped. "I've about reached my limit for gentlemanly restraint."

How far? Amid the brilliant haze of arousal, Sheri contemplated his question. To the moon and back! her mind shouted. And even that might not be far enough. She opened her mouth to tell him, but a sharp electronic beep startled her into silence.

Mark's response leaned more toward the profane as he used one hand to pull the pager from his belt. "Of all the rotten timing!" he added, tossing the thing onto the counter after silencing it.

Sheri collected her whirling thoughts and silently seconded his opinion. "Do you have to call in?"

Mark nodded and swore again. "This is one of those times I wish I wasn't head of a division."

Jealousy pierced her like an emerald blade, making her feel suddenly naked and vulnerable. She pulled away from him to search for her discarded sweater. "Oh? Have you been interrupted like this often?"

Mark chuckled and gathered her back into his arms. "No, Miss Green Eyes. But I'm flattered that you care." When she refused to look at him, he placed a gentle kiss upon her brow. "To tell the truth, I've never been interrupted quite like this before. But maybe it's just as well.... Hey, quit trying to pull away like that! I only meant I wasn't exactly prepared to provide for your protection if we'd gone any further. Were you?"

Belatedly, her sense of self-preservation kicked in. What had she been thinking of? She didn't have anything in the house....

"Apparently not," Mark commented dryly. He bent to retrieve her discarded sweater and helped her pull it on. "Actually I'm glad you don't. I'd rather not think of you as being ready for something like this to happen just anytime." He straightened away from her with a sigh. "Now could I use your telephone? If I don't call in, they'll keep paging me until I do."

Sheri nodded and gestured with one hand toward the wall phone, then picked up their forgotten mugs. "Would you like me to reheat the coffee?"

"Yeah, but hold off on the liqueurs. I might end up working tonight."

His prediction proved correct. He was needed at headquarters immediately.

At her front door he turned and drew her close for a deep kiss fraught with longing. "Damn, I hate leaving like this."

Sheri laughed and glanced down at the telltale bulge behind the fly of his jeans. "Do you have time for a cold shower?"

"Very funny." He pinched her chin lightly. "We have some unfinished business to attend to. You'd better believe I'll be prepared next time."

She arched her brows in mock reproof. "Next time? What makes you think there'll be a next time?"

"This," he said, his blunt fingertip tracing lightly over the tight button of her nipple where it strained against the fabric of her sweater. He smiled when he found the other side equally aroused. "And this," he added, gently taking her hand to press it over the front of his jeans for a moment.

He felt hot and incredibly hard beneath her palm. "When?" she whispered, feeling bereft when he backed away from her touch.

"I don't know. Not tonight, but soon." He bent to give her a discouragingly brief kiss. "I'll call you."

As she watched him drive away, she realized she'd never felt more let down in her life. "It's just sexual frustration," she told herself, going back to the kitchen. But that didn't explain the odd emptiness in her heart.

She had almost finished her first liqueur-laced coffee and was contemplating making another when the phone rang, causing her pulse to skip. She answered it with breathless anticipation, but her heart sank when she heard the labored breathing on the other end of the line. "Not you again," she snapped.

"You finked on me," the heavy voice accused. "I told you to come alone and you brung cops. Now you'll never see your car again."

Her temper boiled over. "Now just a minute! I nearly got myself kidnapped tonight. Were those two bozos friends of yours?"

"No. But I wouldn't have let them hurt you."

"I can't tell you how reassuring that is," she retorted. "What about my car?"

"It's too late. I don't trust you no more. You're just like all the rest, thinkin' you can pull a fast one on me. Well, I ain't that dumb. I smelled a cop the minute that dude in the leather jacket walked into the bar."

"Now just a min—" She stopped because the line had gone dead. "Lovely!" The receiver nearly cracked under the force she used to hang it up. "Just lovely." She picked up her mug and headed for the coffeepot. Maybe she'd have several more B-52s. . . .

"Great idea," she muttered, stopping herself. "Then you'll have a hangover to nurse, on top of everything else."

THE FOLLOWING MORNING Sheri called Mark's office number from the back room in her store. When he answered his voice was more gravelly than usual. The sound tickled her senses like fine emery paper. "Sounds like you had a rough night, Sergeant Sampson," she said lightly. "I'm glad I didn't call you." She felt a satisfied grin creep over her face when he didn't stop to ask who was calling.

"It wouldn't have done you any good. I didn't get in till three. Were you going to beg me to come back?"

Her smile turned into a grimace. "Not exactly. My late-night caller struck again. He wasn't too pleased about your presence at the Blue Fox."

"So he was there, too, huh? I'd give anything to know which one he was." Mark laughed humorlessly. "Obviously he wasn't one of the two we hauled in."

"No. And he claims he doesn't know them. Although he did say he wouldn't have let them harm me."

"A chivalrous crook. Now I've heard it all."

"Not quite," she amended dryly. "He said I'll never get my car back now, because he can't trust me. He made it sound as if I'd betrayed him. Can you believe that?"

This time his laughter rippled with amusement. "Actually it does make a weird kind of sense. And if it means he'll stop bothering you, I'm glad it happened. Your car can be replaced—you can't." A significant pause stretched across the line between them before he added, "I found an open drugstore on the way to work this morning."

Sheri felt her stomach do a slow dip and slide, and a glowing warmth raced along her veins. "Oh." She searched frantically for something else to say, but nothing came to mind.

"That 'oh' sounded kind of tentative. Please don't tell me you're having second thoughts. I still haven't recovered from last night's disappointment."

Was she having second thoughts? Giving in to the white-hot passion of the evening before had been so easy, but discussing it in the prosaic light of morning was another matter. She laughed uneasily and said, "Not second thoughts exactly. I'm just not very adept at coolly planning assignations. I know you'll probably find this hard to believe after last night, but sex has never been a casual thing for me."

"Last night was anything but casual, Sheri." His voice had taken on a sexy drawl. "And I'm not in the habit of planning assignations myself. I just wanted you to know I care enough about you to make sure you're protected when we do make love."

The warmth and sincerity of this words sent a quick thrill through her, obliterating doubt. "Is that going to happen soon?" she asked breathlessly.

"As soon as I can arrange it. Unfortunately, that may be a while. I'm plowed under at work today. And tonight isn't possible, either. After being out so late last night, I promised my daughter I'd spend the evening with her."

Instead of disappointment, admiration blossomed in her heart, and right behind it came another, more startling realization. Something beyond passion stirred her soul, and it felt a lot like love. The mere thought made her heart pound, and she reached out to steady herself against a nearby shelf. Dimly she heard Mark utter a soft oath.

"I'm sorry. That didn't sound much like a man who can't wait to make love to you, did it? The truth is, I was sorely tempted to put April off for another night."

Realizing he'd misinterpreted her silence, she hastened to reassure him. "Don't apologize. I would've given anything to have a father like you when I was a little girl."

"Thanks, but that doesn't do much for my aching libido."

Sheri laughed. "We'll have to take care of that another time." Several customers came in the front door and she had to end the call with a hurried, "Oops, I've got to run. Talk to you soon."

IN THE SMALL CUBICLE he called an office, Mark hung up the telephone and felt his spirits start a downward slide. Damn, he wanted to see her again. And not just for sex, although that was a priority, he admitted. But it went beyond desire. Lately he'd begun to realize he enjoyed just being with her, talking with her . . . even arguing. The air seemed to have an extra zing whenever she was around.

"Dangerous talk," he muttered to himself, picking up a detective's report and trying to concentrate on it. Having an affair was one thing, but he'd be a damned fool to become dependent on her.

"DID I MESS UP the spaghetti sauce, Dad?" April peered at Mark from the other side of the dinner table, her brown eyes anxious behind the large lenses of her glasses.

With an effort, Mark pulled himself from his brooding thoughts. This was supposed to be their special time together; he shouldn't be thinking about Sheri. He picked up his fork and smiled at his daughter around the bright, if slightly lopsided, arrangement of silk flowers in the center of the table—April's latest attempt at interior decorating. "No, honey. The sauce is great, better than the last time we made it."

"Then why did you look so grouchy?" She bent over her plate and began the laborious process of twining pasta onto her fork.

"Sorry, I was thinking about something else."

"Maybe you should take that lady named Sheri out to dinner again. You looked kinda happy when you got home the other night." She paused dramatically, the overloaded fork halfway to her mouth. "Jenny Lee Simpson says her daddy is grouchy a lot when he doesn't have a girlfriend, especially the kind that spends the night."

Mark tried to hide his consternation. The accuracy of his daughter's assumption didn't bother him half as much as the idea of her analyzing his love life, or lack of one. "What else does Jenny Lee Simpson say?" he asked carefully.

April's shoulders lifted slightly under her pink Minnie Mouse sweatshirt. "Oh, she wishes her dad would get married again. She said she liked it better before her mom and dad got divorced."

"When was that?"

"About two years ago, I guess. Before she came into my class at school." She munched solemnly on a piece of garlic bread before adding, "I told her I didn't need a mother, 'cause I have you."

Mark nodded, his throat too tight for speech. The kid had a talent for getting to him when he least expected it. Her unquestioning love and trust sometimes left him feeling terribly inadequate. Was he capable of filling the roles of both father and mother for her? And what would he do when she began the inevitable transition from little girl to young woman? If the stories he'd heard were true, there was a lot more to it than learning to cook and shopping for clothes. Yet he didn't intend to tie himself to some woman just because his daughter needed a feminine role model. He caught himself frowning again and pushed the thought from his mind. For the rest of the meal he encouraged April to talk about her schoolwork.

But as they cleared the table and stacked the dishes in the dishwasher, she returned to her earlier subject. "So, are you going to take her out again?"

He paused in the process of scrubbing the sauce pot. "If you mean Sheri, yes, I might." *Hah!* an inner voice mocked. *You can't wait to see her again—preferably in the privacy of her bedroom!*

"Can I meet her, then? Jenny Lee Simpson says her dad always introduces his dates to her."

Mark decided to keep his opinion of Jenny Lee Simpson and her father to himself. "We'll see," he hedged, not liking the uneasy feeling he got when he contemplated the result of introducing his daughter to Sheri O'Reilly's rather flamboyant style. The child showed enough of that on her own already.

His eyes strayed to the living room, where April's influence could be plainly seen. Against the bland backdrop of beiges and browns there were bright spots of color. Toss pillows in bright primary hues nestled against the couch and armchairs. She'd talked him into buying those the time she'd broken her arm, claiming she needed something soft to rest her cast on.

A fat free-form candle done in scarlet and orange graced the center of the utilitarian coffee table, a questionable tribute to their one foray into the craft of candle making. And an arrangement of brilliantly dyed feathers—a Girl Scout project—decorated the mantel over his granite-faced fireplace.

Not that he disliked the effect, he amended, following April into the living room when the kitchen chores were completed. After all, it was her home, too. And her little touches livened the place up, just as her personality added joy to his life. He just didn't want her to go overboard as her mother had. The apartment he'd shared with Melanie had been a nightmare of discordant colors and patterns, all of which she'd proclaimed superior to his plebeian taste. And then she'd proclaimed his masculinity inferior, too, in the most debasing way she could devise.

"Come on, Dad. You promised to play Boggle." April's impatient voice pulled him back to the comfort of his current home. She might have inherited her looks and taste for bright colors from Melanie, but the child's tenacity had come from him, Mark thought with a smile.

They'd just begun a second round of the game when that tenacity appeared again. "Say, Dad. I've got a great idea. Why don't you ask Sheri to come with us to the Reyeses' beach party? Uncle Lou said you could invite anyone you wanted. And that way I'd get to meet her, too." A beatific smile lighted her face.

Mark felt as if he'd just been outmaneuvered by an expert. "Did Lou put you up to this?"

April bent her head over the small plastic game pieces with a suspicious intensity. "N-no."

Mark knew evasion when he heard it. "Try again."

"Well, you remember last Saturday when he took me and his nieces out to get an ice cream? I think he said it would be nice if you brought someone . . . like Sheri."

That sounded like Lou, Mark thought, shaking his head. "I get the feeling I'm being manipulated, but I guess there's no harm in asking her."

"Neat!" The game pieces went flying in all directions as she flung herself into his arms for a hug. After only a brief squeeze, however, she angled back to look at him, an almost calculating look in her eyes. "Uh, Dad. There's just one more thing—the other kids are bringing their skateboards. Do you think I could have one again?"

He set his lips. "Absolutely not. I told you the last time you asked, no more skateboards. A concussion and a broken arm were enough to convince me."

"Aw, Dad!" April started to pout, then apparently thought better of it. "In that case, I sure hope Sheri says she'll come. I'm going to be awfully bored sitting around while all the other kids are riding their skateboards."

Mark groaned and gave her an affectionate little shake. "Quit trying to lay a guilt trip on me. I'm only thinking of your welfare."

SHERI CAME OUT of a long exhilarating twirl, zills pinging together wildly as the music built to a soul-wrenching crescendo. The last strains died away and she slid into a graceful bow, but her head popped up when the chime of the doorbell broke the silence. "Phooey," she muttered, grabbing a towel from the wooden floor of her spare bedroom. "It's probably a door-to-door salesman." She glanced at her reflection in the room's one mirrored wall. Perspiration dampened her sleeveless bright pink leotard, and the long purple chiffon scarf tied around her hips clung to her legs here and there. Muttering to herself about the inconveniences of free enterprise, she ran to her bedroom, pulled on a short terry robe and headed down the hall.

She yanked open the door, expecting a stranger. Instead Mark Sampson stood on her doorstep, looking sexier than any man had a right to look at two o'clock in the afternoon. The sun wove shimmering gold into his hair, and the color of his eyes rivaled the clear sky above. He wore a crisp white shirt that made his tan seem deeper, and his black jeans looked as if they'd been custom-made.

"Hi! I dropped by your store and your brother said you'd taken the afternoon—" He broke off, his gaze falling to the gap in her robe, which she'd forgotten to tie securely. The front of her clinging leotard was clearly visible, the taut, damp material and daring French cut leaving no question unanswered about undergarments—or lack thereof. He swallowed, apparently with some difficulty. "Uh, I guess you were busy."

Sheri felt as if she'd just been overdosed with a potent aphrodisiac. Good grief, how could the man do that to her with one look? Where it had been warm before, her skin now burned. And her insides felt as if she were filled to the brim with hot, fizzing champagne. "I was rehearsing," she said in a soft, trembly voice, then remembered her manners and added, "Would you like to come in?"

An unabashedly wicked smile deepened the grooves bracketing his mouth, and the gleam in his eyes had nothing to do with the bright afternoon sun. "Sweetheart, that's the best offer I've had all century."

7

SHERI WATCHED Mark close and lock her front door, not sure if the hammering of her heart came more from excitement or anxiety. Surely he hadn't taken time off just to . . . ?

He turned and gave her another one of those slow, sexy smiles. The atmosphere in the hallway grew thick with expectancy. "I decided to play hooky when your brother said you'd taken the afternoon off." He patted his wide leather belt. "See? No pager."

Sheri nodded, an absurd trickle of panic running down her spine. Regardless of her age and experience, she still couldn't manage to feel glib about approaching deep intimacy. Playing the seductress was easy when she danced, but without the music and fantasy she fell prey to uncertainty. "I'm sorry I'm such a mess," she said, gesturing vaguely at her untidy ponytail and damp clothing. "I really should shower and change. Would you like to wait in the living room? I could get you a soda or some coffee. . . ." She let the words trail off, realizing how ridiculously nervous she sounded.

Mark shook his head and moved toward her until she was backed against the wall. "What I'd like," he said, touching a blunt fingertip to the tendrils of dark hair curling around her ear, "is to see you dance again. Just for me. Would you do that?"

"But I'm not dressed for—"

His fingertip pressed against her lips, halting her protest. "You look terrific." He nudged her chin up and the warmth of his mouth came against hers in sweet persuasion. "Please dance for me, Scheherazade. I've dreamed about it ever since that first night." Urgency vibrated in every word, driving away her doubts, filling her with an irresistible need to fulfill his dream.

Silently she took his hand and led him to her rehearsal room. At the door she paused, gesturing toward the single piece of furniture, a dark burgundy futon. "You can sit there, if you like. I...I'll set up the music."

Mark touched the switch on the wall. "Do you mind if I turn this off?" She shook her head and the overhead light went out, leaving the room with only the muted gold of daylight that managed to filter through the coarse weave of the heavy draperies.

Sheri selected a tape and slipped it into the small stereo system set up in one corner. Facing the mirrored wall, she shrugged off the terry robe, then scooped up the gossamer white veil she'd left on the floor. Her hands shook a little as she wrapped the material around her. She had danced before more men than she could remember, large crowds and small, but none of those times had made her feel as anxious and vulnerable as she was now.

She moved slowly to the center of the polished floor and waited for the music to begin, her eyes downcast. The piece she'd selected was a personal favorite, one she'd never performed in public, for a very basic reason. "Desert Serenade" pulsed with a primal sensuality that called to the wanton side of her nature, and she knew it showed in her dancing.

The music began, unfurling in a liquescent wave that stirred her soul. Slowly, slowly she raised her eyes to meet the gaze of the man comfortably sprawled on the futon's long cushions. The music wrapped around her, its dulcet call luring her body into the first gentle movements of seduction.

The veil swished softly over her body, and the clinging fit of her leotard made her feel as if she were dancing naked. *A harem girl*, an inner voice whispered fancifully. *Dancing to lure her master into her bed for the night.* The illusion beckoned and she let her eyelids droop until she viewed Mark through a screen of lashes. A blond, blue-eyed sheik? Why not? The coloring might be wrong, but his lean tough look certainly fit the bill. Dressed in keffiyeh and djellaba ... The image made her smile dreamily, and the smile Mark sent back to her seemed to glow with the self-satisfaction of an Arab prince surveying his property.

Sheri experienced a queer sense of déjà vu, as if she'd once known how it felt to be possessed that way. It filled her with a need to retaliate, an elemental drive

as old as womankind to temper masculine domi-
nance with desire.

The music swelled and sighed, a melodic co-con-
spirator in the provocative movements of her body.
She moved closer to the futon, the veil slipping to the
floor as her body swayed in a flowing invitation.
*Come to me, my love. Let me feed the fires of your
passion.*

She was close enough to touch him now, close
enough to see the burning response in his eyes, the
sensual softening of his beautiful mouth, the rapid rise
and fall of his chest. And lower, unlike the flowing
folds of a djellaba, his snug jeans revealed the most
basic reaction of all.

*I want to love you, beautiful dancer, I want to be
deep inside you, feeling you tight and warm around
me. And I want to stay there forever.*

Sheri inhaled a shuddering breath and stumbled a
step at the force of his unspoken words. In an instant
Mark was beside her, steadying her with strong
hands.

"Sheri . . ." His voice came out raw and rasping. "I
don't know how much more I can take."

"Nor do I," she whispered, reaching to clasp his face
with trembling hands. "Please, Mark, make love to
me."

He accepted the invitation without hesitation. With
a low moan he claimed her mouth in a searing kiss,
his tongue delving deep then withdrawing, coaxing
her response. She complied eagerly, exploring the

slick warmth inside his mouth as he held her prisoner there with a gentle suction. She felt him hook his fingers under the straps of her leotard and ease them down, peeling the fabric from her breasts. Then he worked on the buttons of his shirt until it parted and she experienced the first sweet shock of naked flesh meeting naked flesh.

The light mat of hair on his chest abraded the tips of her breasts, teasing her until she thought she would go mad. She pushed his shirt completely off and tugged at the buckle of his belt. When it resisted her efforts, Mark took over and within moments he stood before her, golden-tanned and gloriously aroused. She only had a brief look before he bent to pull down her leotard and the scarf at her hips until she could step out of them. Then his arms swept her close again and the rigid heat of his erection burned against her stomach. So strong, so potent . . .

A dim warning sounded in her brain, and she pulled back to look at him. "Did you bring . . . ?"

"You'd better believe it, sweetheart." He led her to the futon and eased her down before turning away to reach for his jeans. "I stuffed my pockets."

Caught in the bewitching ebb and flow of the music she watched with burning fascination as he dealt with the contents of the filmy plastic package.

Moments later he leaned over her, his features taut with desire. "You drive me wild when you dance. It makes me want to do the same for you." He bent to kiss her lips, and his hand closed over her breast. She moaned as he lazily dragged his lips down the tender arch of her throat, down to the softness of her breasts. She cried out, her pulse echoing the throbbing beat that filled the room as the hot, moist suction of his mouth captured first one tender nipple, then the other.

"Do you want me, Sheri?" he inquired roughly. "Are you hurting like I am?" His hand smoothed the tight skin from her rib cage to the slight swell of her belly and moved lower still. She gasped and shivered at the gentle probing of his fingertips. He slid deep, deeper, testing her readiness.

"Oh, babe, what a welcome," he whispered. "You're all hot and wet, just for me." He eased himself onto the cushions and she opened to him, loving the feel of his hard body pressing her thighs wider. And then she felt the delicious penetration begin, stretching her, filling her completely. When it was done, he let out a guttural sigh and lifted his head to meet her unfocused gaze, his blue eyes appearing clouded with desire.

Destiny, she thought, her senses reeling. This had been preordained from the first time she'd shared his impassioned thoughts. But the dream paled beside the blazing pleasure of reality.

"I've wanted this from the first night I saw you dance," Mark said, his voice low, strained. "To feel your soft, seductive body beneath me, closing around me so warm, so tight..." He withdrew to thrust again and again, building his tempo in time to the inciting fantasia that played on in the background.

Sheri reached up to grip the hard curve of his shoulders and followed his rhythm as naturally as she followed the music, her body arching and tightening as it did when she danced.

Another harsh sound came from deep in Mark's chest. "Do you know what it feels like when you do that? I may die from it." He gasped and swore softly when she repeated the motion. "I'll take the risk. Do it again."

She tried to laugh, but shuddering contractions seized her unawares, ripping a startled cry from her throat. The sensation went on and on, burning hotter and fiercer until she thought she couldn't bear it. Somewhere in the midst of it all she felt Mark grow rigid and heard his sharp exclamation of release. Their bodies convulsed together, the world seemed to explode, and in the hazy aftermath she heard the echoes of her own frantic little scream.

Time seemed of little consequence as she lay there dazed and spent beneath Mark's equally inert form. She could feel the warm rush of his breath against her neck, still a little forced from the exertion. Just thinking about it caused a small aftershock. She wrapped her arms around his lean torso, savoring the weight of his body, wanting to hold him there forever.

What would he do if he knew she'd fallen in love with him? He'd said he cared for her, desired her, but that didn't mean he was ready for love. Especially considering the way he'd been burned in his previous marriage. A pinprick of anxiety invaded her sweet lassitude.

As if he sensed her distress, Mark moaned and levered himself up on his forearms, then shifted his body and rolled to a sitting position.

Sheri uttered a small sound of protest and opened her eyes to search his expression. Even in profile he looked disgruntled. Hadn't he enjoyed their lovemaking as much as she?

"Why are you looking at me like that?" He eyed her over his shoulder while casually dispensing with the means of her protection.

Taken aback, she turned her head away. "I guess I didn't expect you to be so eager to get away from me." She gave him a challenging glance. "And you don't exactly look pleased at the moment."

He slid back onto the cushion facing her and bent to brush his mouth against hers. "That isn't your fault. I'm just a little unhappy with the method of birth control we're using. I wanted to stay inside you, but it's too risky. If it wasn't, I'd still be there."

Relief bubbled up inside her like a clear mountain spring. "Does that mean you aren't leaving for a while?"

He grinned and nibbled on her lower lip. "Once I've found your bedroom, you'll have a hard time getting rid of me. Did I remember to tell you how much I enjoyed your dancing?" He leaned lower and gave her shoulder a less gentle nip. "Or how insanely jealous it makes me feel to think of any other man seeing you like that?"

Sheri gasped at the small punishment and grabbed twin handfuls of his thick silky hair. "I don't dance like that for other men," she said, giving his head a shake. "In fact, I rarely do public appearances anymore. I don't have the time since I opened my business."

He frowned. "What about that bachelor party the night we met?"

"That was an exception. I did it as a favor to Lou, because his sister is my friend." After what had just happened, she couldn't imagine ever again performing in front of a roomful of strange men. The realization gave her pause, and she decided to keep it to herself for the time being.

Mark let out a long, slow breath and reached to smooth back her tousled bangs. "I know I don't have any right to say this, but I'm glad."

Sheri experienced a fresh twinge of unease and wondered why the first part of his admission bothered her. She certainly didn't want a man who felt he could run her life; she'd had enough of that with her ex-husband. But she sensed a distancing in Mark's words, a deliberate setting of boundaries. She wanted to ask him about it, but the hand that had been stroking her hair began to chart more stimulating territory, and his eyes had that entrancing smoky-blue cast again. "Why don't you show me where your bedroom is? I don't think I can take another round on this thing." He rose and helped her to her feet. "It's a miracle we didn't fall off the last time."

Sheri chuckled and led him down the hall, wondering what he'd have to say when he saw her bed.

"I FEEL like some kind of sultan," Mark declared a good while later as he surveyed the scarlet and royal-blue draperies tenting her water bed. Soft track lighting both inside and outside the canopy provided glowing illumination against the encroaching darkness of early evening.

"Is that a complaint?" Sheri demanded after swallowing a bite of pizza. Sensual hunger temporarily sated, they were sitting on her bed sharing a large pepperoni and artichoke heart creation—the artichokes confined to her side. Her only concession to propriety was Mark's shirt, which she wore with the sleeves rolled up. Mark, who had gone to the door earlier to pay the delivery boy, wore only his jeans.

Mark thought about her question and grinned. "Not exactly. It just takes getting used to." He bounced a little, jiggling the water-filled mattress. "And I'm not so sure I wouldn't get seasick if I tried to sleep on this thing."

"You didn't mind the motion a little while ago," Sheri replied meaningfully. She set down her slice of pizza and regarded him, hands on hips. "Was your reference to the mattress a subtle way of asking to spend the night?"

Mark made a grimace of regret. "I wish I could, but that would mean getting a sitter for April, and I have to leave her often enough when I'm called to the field at night."

Sheri tried not to let her disappointment show. After all, his obvious dedication to his daughter was one of the things that made her love him. But she still didn't want him to leave.

Mark shoved the pizza box aside and pulled her onto his lap. "Don't look at me like that. I wish there were some way I could be with both of you at once." He paused as if considering, then cleared his throat. "I was going to ask you to go to the Reyeses' beach party with me and April on Saturday, but I suppose you'll be tied up at your shop."

Something about the way he asked bothered her. Was it the hesitation? The thread of unease in his voice? But it faded to insignificance next to her growing need just to be with him. "Quit anticipating what I will or won't do," she ordered, giving him a gentle cuff on the chin for emphasis. "Tina already asked me if I could come and I told her I wasn't sure. But since you're asking, I'll try a little harder to arrange it. Everything depends on whether or not Sean will agree to mind the store." Her mouth twisted ruefully. "The odds of that are pretty good, considering his usual work schedule."

She saw Mark's eyes narrow in sudden perception. "That bothers you, doesn't it? You defend his right to be what he is, but you really would like to see him become something more."

Unable to deny his claim, Sheri averted her eyes and reached for the wineglass she'd left on the bedside table. "I just hate to see him let all his intelligence and education go to waste. He could contribute so much." She sipped the wine, letting the burgundy's robust flavor bloom on her tongue, then offered the glass to Mark.

He took a quick drink and set the glass down on the table. "Yet you were ready to jump all over me, just because I looked a little surprised when I found out what he did. Why?"

She gave him an indignant look. "Because he's my brother. Why else?" When he didn't reply immediately, she squirmed off his lap and sat back on her heels, arms akimbo.

Mark frowned and gestured impatiently. "Hey, it's nothing to get upset about. I simply thought that being separated from your brother all those years would have made you less interdependent. It's a natural assumption. Why are you so defensive about it?"

Sheri stopped to consider that. *Was* she being overly sensitive? Or had she detected an underlying message in his assumption? Was it possibly wishful thinking on his part that she had no need for commitment and permanent attachments, because he had no desire for them himself? She decided to test the waters.

"I might be a little defensive, but only because I've had to work so hard all my life to have any kind of family ties. If anything, separation from my brother made the idea more important to me. Maybe that's why I tried so hard to please my grandmother for so many years. Maybe that's why I wasted so much time trying to become the woman my ex-husband wanted me to be. The bottom line is—" she paused and looked directly into his eyes "—I tend to seek long-term relationships."

Mark shifted uncomfortably and rubbed the back of his neck with one hand. "Is that what you expect of me?" The look he gave her was filled with uncertainty and maybe a touch of regret. "If so, I can't make any promises at this point."

She ducked her head, determined not to let him see how much it mattered to her, then realized he must have seen. With an impatient sound, he caught her hands and tumbled her onto the buoyant mattress. When she tried to twist away, he pulled her close until they lay on their sides face-to-face. He gazed at her for a long moment, then rested his forehead against hers and closed his eyes.

"I'm sorry if that hurt you, but I was only trying to be honest. You have to understand, Sheri. Relationships are difficult for me." He raised his hand to stroke the sensitive nape of her neck, toying with the fine curls that had pulled free from her ponytail. "Would it help to know that I care more deeply for you than I have for any woman in a long time? Or that I'm still a little rocky from the power of our lovemaking?"

Yes, it did help, she told herself, cherishing the promise in his admission. His fingertip delicately traced the shell of her ear and a sensual tremor swept through her when he added, "How about if I told you I want to do it again already, even after four times in as many hours?"

"Five, if you count the time in the shower," she corrected with a shivery little laugh. *It's going to be all right*, she told herself. *Just give him a little time*.

"Care to make it six?" Mark inquired, his fingers deftly undoing the shirt covering her breasts.

"Wh-what about your daughter?" she gasped, her hands already seeking the wonderful contours of his lean, tightly muscled chest.

"I'll tell her I had to put in a little overtime. She'll understand." He pulled the shirt off her shoulders and began raining light, tantalizing kisses over the rounded swell of her breasts. "Especially if I tell her you're coming to the beach party with us. She's anxious to meet you."

Sheri smiled, telling herself she must have imagined the hesitation in his earlier invitation. "The feeling's mutual," she declared, pulling him close.

THE FOLLOWING SATURDAY proved to be one of those spring days that made San Diego such a popular vacation spot for freezing Midwesterners. The temperature hovered in the high seventies, and not one cloud marred the azure sky as Mark guided the Bronco toward Mission Bay Park. *Everything's perfect,* he told himself. So why did he feel as if disaster were lurking just around the corner?

He eyed his daughter, who was practically hanging herself on her seat belt to lean back and chatter to Sheri. No problem there. The two of them had hit it off from the instant they'd laid eyes on each other. Sheri obviously enjoyed children and had a way of listening and responding that brought out April's natural talkativeness. He should have been happy they were getting along so well. Instead his uneasiness deepened. By the time they reached the park, he had begun to feel like a fifth wheel.

"Is something wrong?" Sheri asked quietly as she helped him unload the picnic gear. April had dashed off to join the assortment of Reyes children already gathered in the park's playground area. "You hardly said a word in the car."

Mark forced a wry smile. "I wasn't given much chance. You and April sounded like old chums who haven't seen each other in years."

"She's an adorable child," Sheri admitted with a laugh. "But that doesn't explain why you look so grouchy."

What could he tell her? That the easy camaraderie she seemed to have with his daughter made him nervous? That he didn't like the idea of April becoming too attached to her when he still had reservations? No way; he'd sound like a real jerk. Better to offer a half truth. "I haven't been sleeping too well lately. I have a lot on my mind."

"Really?" She sent him an inquiring look, and he couldn't help thinking how sexy she looked, even with her hair pulled back in a neat French braid. Maybe it was the cuffed white shorts or that T-shirt with the wild impressionistic painting on the front that made him think of pagan rites.

"What has you so upset you can't sleep?" she prompted.

He strode over to her, pressed a hard, fast kiss onto her soft mouth and said, "You."

She let out one breathless "Oh!" then started toward the grassy area under a stand of tall trees, where the Reyes family had cordoned off tables. His picnic basket and her beach bag swung jauntily from her hands.

Following her with the heavy ice chest gripped in front of him, Mark experienced more reservations. Was she aware that every man around had his eyes glued on those long shapely legs of hers? By the time they reached the large group of Lou's relatives, he could barely contain a hot flash of jealousy. Lou didn't help matters when he greeted her with a long, low wolf whistle. Sheri laughed it off, but Mark felt like punching his best friend.

The day progressed downhill from there for Mark. While he tended to approach socializing cautiously, Sheri seemed to become fast friends with everyone there—no mean feat, given the size of the Reyes clan.

Not that she ignored him, but she didn't exactly stay glued to his side, either. He told himself he wouldn't have wanted that; he hated clinging women. But contrarily he resented it.

He made an effort to join in, joking with Lou and his brothers, giving uncounted pushes to the dozens of children playing on the nearby swings, taking his turn at the barbecue to cook the thin marinated steaks called *carne asada*. And at lunch Sheri sat gratifyingly close to him at the long table, sharing his beer as they loaded flour tortillas with the sliced meat, guacamole, tomatoes and cilantro. But beneath his socially acceptable demeanor he continued to brood.

After the meal he got drafted on to Lou's team for a wild game of softball and dived into it wholeheartedly, using the physical exertion to work off some of his inner turmoil. He was half glad, too, when Sheri declined Lou's invitation to play, claiming she'd rather to go off exploring with April and the other children for a while. Mark knew he wouldn't have been able to concentrate on his playing with her nearby.

The game proved to be good therapy. He could feel the tension easing out of his body each time he raced around the bases or launched himself high to catch a fly ball.

Lou's team was ahead by six runs, and Mark had just tagged a runner out when one of Lou's young nephews came tearing toward the sandy area where they were playing. "Mr. Sampson!" he hollered.

"Come quick! April fell off a skateboard and hurt herself!"

Mark's heart constricted. He took off at a dead run, following the child toward a section of the park where there were wide concrete walks. He shouldered his way through the small crowd that had gathered and saw Sheri kneeling to support the shoulders of a pale and shaken April, who lay sprawled on the hard surface. Through the panic roaring in his ears he dimly heard Sheri's gently encouraging words, ordering his daughter to relax and breathe slowly.

"What happened?" he demanded roughly.

Sheri looked up, her eyes full of dismay. "I'm sorry, Mark, she fell. The kids talked me into trying one of their skateboards, and I didn't think—"

"I'm sure you didn't," he snarled, cutting off her excuse. He should have known she would be involved—she seemed to attract misadventure. Sliding his arm around April's shoulders, he pushed Sheri's arm out of the way. "I'll take over from here." He turned to his daughter, but not fast enough to miss the hurt in Sheri's expression. Shoving the image from his mind, he focused his attention on comforting April, who looked as if she were going to burst into tears.

He didn't look up until Lou's older sister Rita arrived and knelt beside him, announcing she was a nurse. Within a short while she had gotten the details of the accident from the other children and given April a thorough check.

"I think she just had the wind knocked out of her," Rita pronounced, giving Mark's arm a reassuring squeeze. "She didn't hit her head, and there don't appear to be any sprains or broken bones. Give her a few minutes to catch her breath, and she'll probably be tearing around with the rest of the kids again."

"Thanks," Mark replied roughly. He scooped April up and carried her to a shady place under the trees.

"Daddy, don't be mad," April pleaded, as he lowered her to the blanket Sheri had spread out earlier.

He grasped April's chin and gave her a gentle shake. "I'm not as mad as I am scared. Stay put and I'll get you a drink of water."

Out of the corner of his eye he saw Sheri approaching as he filled a cup from the drinking fountain. "If you're going to apologize again or offer more excuses, don't bother," he snapped when she reached him. "It was bad enough when you involved me in your wild stunts, but to risk my daughter's safety is too much." Water sloshed out of the cup onto his shoes as he swung toward her.

Anger darkened her hazel eyes to a fierce green. "Now just a minute. I didn't force the child to get on that thing."

"You must have given her permission, and that's as bad. April had specific orders from me about not skateboarding. The only reason I can think of for her to disobey me is that you told her it would be okay."

Sheri propped her hands on her hips. "I have a news flash for you, mister. She didn't ask for my permission. As I tried to tell you earlier, I didn't even think she intended to try it. Although if you want my opinion, I don't see why she shouldn't. Lots of kids ride skateboards."

"And lots of them get hurt. April got a broken arm and concussion from her last ride before this one."

Sheri threw out her hands in exasperation. "Hey, kids get hurt all the time, doing all sorts of things. It's part of growing up."

In a calmer moment he might have agreed with her. But coming on top of the fright he'd just had and his earlier annoyance, it sounded as if she were attacking his competence as a father. "I don't need your advice on child rearing," he said between clenched teeth. "So far I've taken care of my daughter quite well without the help of you or anyone else."

Sheri jerked back as if he'd struck her and her expression reflected a dawning realization. "And that's the way you intend for it to stay, isn't it? There isn't room in your life for me, except perhaps for the occasional afternoon dalliance? In your eyes that's all I'm good for."

"Damn it, you're putting words in my mouth again."

Her eyes glittered with a suspicious moisture. "Am I? Or am I simply stating what you haven't admitted to yourself yet?"

That stopped him cold. Could there be some truth in what she said? Was that what had been bothering him all day, the aspect of making room for her in the life he shared with April?

"I'm right, aren't I?" Choking on the last word, she whirled and strode away from him.

"Wait a minute," he called, loping after her, more water spilling from the forgotten cup in his hand. "Where are you going?"

"Home." She snatched her purse from the blanket where April sat. "Goodbye, sweetheart. It was great meeting you. I hope you're feeling better soon."

"How are you going to get home?" Mark demanded, nearly tossing the glass of water—what remained of it—to his daughter. "I drove, remember?"

"This city has an excellent transportation system. I'll manage." She gave him a tight little smile, most likely for April's sake. "Goodbye, Mark. It's been...educational knowing you." With a regal lift of her chin, she turned and stalked off toward the street.

Watching her go, Mark could feel the attention of every person there focused on him. But when he looked back at his daughter, he encountered the most censorious gaze of all.

"If you don't go make up with her, I'll never speak to you again," April announced, her eyes brimming with tears.

8

CAUGHT IN A MAELSTROM of fury and hurt and self-reproach, Sheri leaned against the post of the bus-stop sign, arms tightly wrapped across her middle. How could she have been so blind, so naive? Mark Sampson had never intended to let her into his life. Heaven knows, she thought, she'd had enough signs; he'd even told her he wasn't ready for anything permanent. What a dope she'd been.

A car horn beeped and she looked up, just as Tina's blue sports car screeched to a halt in front of her. The top was down and Tina gestured toward the passenger seat. "Come on, I'll give you a lift home."

Sheri shook her head. "I can use the long bus ride. I have a lot of thinking to do and I don't want to discuss a certain male of previous acquaintance."

Tina made a dismissive gesture with one hand. "I always think better when I'm riding in a car with the top down. It clears the head." She leaned over and opened the passenger door. "If it's time you need, I'll take the long road home. And we won't talk about Mark Sampson unless you want to."

Sheri stood her ground a moment, then slid into the seat, telling herself it was easier than standing there arguing until the next bus came. The nimble little car roared off at once, and Sheri leaned her head back and let the crisp ocean breeze buffet her face. The piercing hurt of Mark's rejection gradually lessened to a heavy ache in her heart, and the heat of her anger died out, leaving her with nothing but cold misery.

Tina drove silently, taking the scenic route north past the coastal towns of La Jolla and Del Mar. As they cruised along the colorful montage of exotic shops, elegant high-rise condominiums and lush Southern California flora, soothing music came from the car's tape deck, eliminating the need for small talk. It wasn't until they stopped for a glass of wine at a beach restaurant that Sheri broke the silence.

Once they were settled, she touched her glass to Tina's in a small toast. "Thanks for being so understanding about what happened back there at the picnic. I can imagine what your family must be thinking." She shook her head and sat back to gaze at the ocean's choppy sun-gilded waves.

Tina grinned. "Hey, we all know about lovers' quarrels."

Sheri paused with the wineglass halfway to her lips. "What makes you think we're lovers?"

"The expression on Mark's face every time one of the other guys dared to glance your way." Tina smiled and tossed her dark hair back from her shoulders. "He turned greener than my guacamole dip. The man has it bad for you."

"Lust maybe, but not love." Sheri shook her head and tasted her wine. "He made it quite clear today that I didn't meet his standards for full participation in his life—especially involvement with his daughter."

"Did he actually say that?" When Sheri nodded, Tina sighed. "I think he just needs time to get used to the idea of sharing April. I saw how well you got along with her today. Remember right after lunch, when she asked you to French-braid her hair so it would look like yours? And then she made that remark about her father not being able to do it? Mark looked as if he'd been tried and convicted of being a lousy parent."

Sheri let out a slow, weary breath. "She's such an adorable child, I couldn't help falling in love with her." *Any more than I could help falling in love with her father*, she added silently. "I never dreamed it would bother him."

"I don't think it's a permanent problem. He just needs time to realize you aren't going to steal April away from him."

Sheri shook her head from side to side. "I wish it were as simple as that." She caught herself on the verge of saying more and pulled back. "You're a wonderful friend, Tina, but you just don't understand the full scope of the situation." She took another sip of her wine and set down the glass on the table. "I think we should start back to my place now. I have a million things to do before the jazz concert at the café tomorrow night."

Tina nodded, acknowledging that the subject had been politely closed. They hardly spoke at all on the ride back to Sheri's house.

Sheri had retreated to brooding silence by the time they turned onto her street. But a shot of irritation brought her around quickly enough when she saw the Bronco parked in her driveway.

"Looks like you have company," Tina quipped, pulling to the curb.

Reluctantly, Sheri slipped out of the car and gave Tina an exasperated glance. "I don't want to talk to him right now. Could you come in for a while?"

"Sorry, but I just recalled an appointment I'm late for," Tina said with a guilty grin. The car began to move away from the curb. "Remember what I said about giving him time."

Muttering to herself about people who deserted friends in a time of need, Sheri turned and started up the walk. She pointedly ignored Mark, who got out of the Bronco and followed.

"We have to talk," he announced as she jammed the key into the door's lock and gave it a vicious twist.

She spun around and glared at him. "About what? Setting up a schedule for our little afternoon trysts? Or is this to be like the conversation I once had with my ex-husband? The one where he outlined all the defects of my personality that he expected me to change if I wanted him to stop being unfaithful to me. Or perhaps you'd like to point out again my unsuitability as a companion for your daughter, or the disastrous effects of my unorthodox upbringing?" She jerked back to the door, shoved it open and stomped inside. When Mark followed, she whirled once again, more angry words ready. But he stopped her with an upheld hand.

"I'm not here for any of those reasons. I simply wanted to tell you how sorry I am about what happened today." He pushed the door closed and locked it with a snap of his wrist.

She tossed her purse onto the hall table and leaned back against it, arms crossed. "Being sorry isn't enough, Mark. We're dealing with a major life-style conflict here. Or, to be more specific, you don't approve of mine."

"I did some thinking about that and a few other things while I waited for you." He gave her a wry look. "Fortunately for me, Tina decided to take the long way back here, so I had lots of time." He shoved his hands into the back pockets of his slacks and glanced down at his feet. "I left the picnic not long after you did. It seems I'd worn out my welcome there—especially with my daughter."

Momentarily distracted, Sheri asked, "Is she all right? I nearly died when I first saw her lying on that sidewalk. She looked so pale." She lowered her brows threateningly. "I hope you weren't too hard on her. I don't think it was a deliberate act of disobedience. She just wanted to be a part of what her friends were doing. I'll bet even you gave in to peer pressure at least once when you were a kid."

"I guess I did," Mark admitted with a reluctant smile. "And you needn't worry about her, she's fine. In fact she talked me into letting her spend the night with Rita's girls." His expression turned rueful. "If anybody got a hard time, it was me. My daughter told me she'd never speak to me again if I didn't make up with you."

Sheri experienced a strong tug in the region of her heart, but refused to give in to it. "Is that why you're here? To save face with your daughter?"

His blue eyes glinted in the half light of the hall. "No. I'm here because I discovered I can't bear the thought of not seeing you again." He took a step toward her. "I'm here to ask for a chance to explain what happened today."

He closed the remaining distance between them and clasped her elbows, drawing her up until they stood mere millimeters apart. She inhaled sharply, catching the clean beguiling scent of his sun-warmed skin, and felt an unwanted quaver in the pit of her stomach.

"Please say you'll listen, Sheri." The request was gently voiced, but his dark blond eyebrows tightened with concern and a small muscle twitched in his jaw. Even so she felt torn between compassion and caution.

Resisting an urge to reach up and stroke the tension from his brow, she simply said, "All right, we'll talk. But let's do it sitting in the living room." The forced intimacy of the hall was undermining her ability to remain objective. She slipped past him and led the way, deliberately choosing a gold plush armchair facing the couch.

Mark sat on the very edge of the couch, elbows propped on his knees, hands loosely clasped. "I think I'd better tell you about my previous marriage first," he began abruptly. "I'm not sure how much you already know...."

Sheri used a fingertip to trace a pattern on the chair's arm. "I know your ex was a dancer, that you married her when you found out she was pregnant, and that she deserted you when April was still a baby."

"A highly simplified version." Mark studied his hands. "I wasn't completely blameless. I fell hard for Melanie the first time I laid eyes on her. She was beautiful, talented and just reckless enough to be exciting to a green young cop. I knew she didn't want to be tied down to one man, but I still wanted her. I actually believed fortune had smiled on me when her irresponsible attitude toward birth control backfired."

He clenched his hands together, then deliberately relaxed them. "I couldn't have been more wrong. Melanie hated being married almost as much as she hated being pregnant. I never knew where she went or what she did while I was on duty, but she frequently wasn't home when I got there. And after April's birth the situation got worse. Melanie began pursuing her dancing career with a vengeance, dumping April on anyone who'd watch her. Too often I'd come home to an empty house and have no idea where my child was—let alone my wife."

He rose suddenly and began to prowl around the room. "But I was even willing to make allowances for that—until the time I came home and found Melanie there with another man." He stopped to examine a circus poster depicting an old-fashioned lady tightrope walker complete with flounced dress and umbrella. "He was a talent scout from New York. Evidently they were using our bed as the casting couch. I assume she got the part, because she left the following day."

As she had the first time they'd met, Sheri felt the ache of his memory as surely as if it had been her own. But it didn't temper her rising sense of injustice. She didn't need telepathy to see the connection he'd made between her and his ex-wife.

"Mark, I'm sorry you got hurt," she began, keeping her voice even. "But I get the uncomfortable feeling that you're attributing her faults to me. I'm not Melanie."

He glanced back at her and resumed his wandering. "Believe me, I know that. Melanie never had your warmth or compassion. With her it was fire or ice, uncontrolled passion or frozen indifference. But there are some things about you that remind me of her."

Immediately on guard, she inquired quietly, "Such as?"

Mark faced her, his hand resting on the gilt saddle of her carousel horse. "Such as your tendency to rush off after the things you want without considering the consequences. And your propensity for diving head-first into something new without first testing the waters."

Her anger boiled over like an untended pot. "Reckless and irresponsible, is that what you're trying to say?" The force of her temper propelled her out of the chair and across the room to face him.

Mark grimaced in irritation. "No, that isn't it. You're just—"

"Weird? Bohemian? Low-class?" she shot back. "How about unfocused? Or intemperate? Or—" Her voice caught, and she spun away from him to hide the tears that threatened.

His powerful hands caught her shoulders, bringing her back around. "Why do I get the feeling that someone else's words are being shoved down my throat?" He stared at her a moment, and the annoyance creasing his brow eased a bit, giving way to understanding. "I guess it's safe to assume a good portion of that came from your ex-husband."

Sheri shrugged, refusing to look at him until his broad palm caressed her cheek, coaxing her to meet his gaze.

"Sounds like he did a real number on you."

A soft, derisive hiss escaped her. "Everett had a particular gift for character annihilation. My self-esteem hit an all-time low after our divorce." She compressed her lips into a grim little smile. "When my father gave me the 450SL, he told me to make sure Everett saw me in it. I think for a while that car became a symbol of respectability for me."

"Is that why you're so determined to get it back?"

His question startled and annoyed her. "Of course not," she snapped. "I no longer need a car—or a man—to establish my self-worth." At least she hoped that was the case.

"You don't need it to prove your worth to me either." Mark's hands applied a light pressure to her shoulders, but she resisted moving into his arms.

"But what about my impulsiveness, my wild stunts and all the other things about me you don't approve of?" A desperate sadness filled her. "I can't change what I am, Mark. Not for you, not for any man. It's better to end it now, before it gets even more complicated." *Before he finds out you're in love with him,* her heart added.

"I'm not asking you to change," he responded, reaching to frame the curve of her cheek with one hand. "I learned the futility of that while I was with

Melanie. And I probably wouldn't feel the way I do about you if you were different. The very aspects of your personality that worry me are part of what attracted me to you in the first place. That's what I figured out this afternoon while I was waiting for you. Sure, we're different, but I think we have a lot to offer each other if we can learn to overcome our differences—to compromise."

The sincerity in his words reached out to her, but she couldn't give in quite that easily. Everett, too, had spoken of compromise before their marriage; afterward it had been another story. The concept was easy to talk about, but much harder to put into practice. "Mark, you don't know what you're getting into," she said, shaking her head slowly. "You say we can learn to make allowances for each other, but there are things you don't even know about me. Things you might find too outrageous to accept."

"Uh-oh, this sounds serious." Mark's smile indicated he was thinking the opposite. His thumb began to brush lightly against the sensitive underside of her chin, and for a moment her eyes closed in helpless pleasure. "Are you going to tell me you like to go nude sunbathing on Black's Beach?" he prompted in a teasing whisper.

Her eyes popped open. "No! But you'll probably think it's worse than that. It's . . . it's something involving you."

His eyes darkened. "Now you really have me intrigued. Quick, tell me before I get any more ideas."

She looked straight into his eyes and demanded, "What would you say if I told you I've . . . intercepted some of your thoughts occasionally?"

Mark's hand stilled against her throat. "Intercepted? What do you mean?"

"I mean I've known exactly what you've been thinking more than once."

"Are you talking about mind reading?" His voice slid upward in a tone of disbelief.

"Something like that." When she looked at him, his expression had tightened with skepticism. She hadn't expected him to believe it right away, but that didn't make her feel any less defensive. "I'm sure you think I imagined it, but I didn't."

He cleared his throat uneasily. "Okay, when did this supposedly happen?"

"Several times. For instance on the night we met. While I was dancing I knew you were thinking about making love with me."

Mark cracked a grin. "Honey, it wouldn't have taken a mind reader to figure that out. I'd wager most of the men in the room were thinking the same thing."

"Not exactly the same," she insisted. A smile touched her mouth as she recalled just how precise his daydream had been. And even that hadn't been as good as the real thing the other night. . . .

"Tell me about some of the other times," he said, obviously unconvinced.

She complied, but soon realized she was wasting her time. He looked more incredulous with every word. Even the way he shifted away from her to stand propped against the wall radiated indulgent attention rather than a readiness to believe.

Finally she gave up, throwing her hands out in surrender. "I can see you don't believe me." Spinning away from him, she went to the window and pretended to straighten the draperies. She tried to laugh, to cover her disappointment, but managed only an odd hiccuping sound.

"I was right, wasn't I?" she demanded. "You don't really want to become involved with a wacko like me." She heard him cross the room to her, but didn't turn, fearing what she'd see in his eyes.

"In case you haven't noticed, crazy lady," he murmured, wrapping his arms around her from behind, "I already am involved." His breath warmed her nape for an instant before his mouth tasted the tender flesh there. An uncontrollable shudder ran through her.

"Remember what I said about compromise? Is it really important that I believe in the paranormal—as long as I don't object to your belief in it?"

"I guess no—ohh . . ." She broke off on a moan as he nuzzled his way around to the sensitive curve of her throat. Compromise. Was it really possible? The voice of experience said no, but the love burning in her heart cried out for a chance to try.

The imprint of his smile warmed her skin. "I'm glad we agree on that, because I have a much more basic form of communication in mind at the moment." He paused, his arm tightening just below the curve of her breasts. "Unless, of course, you have other plans."

Sheri wavered a moment more, but cool-headed reason was no match for the compelling warmth of his embrace. Knowing full well the risk she was taking, she decided to follow the urging of her heart and eased around to face him. "If I did have plans, I'd change them." In the next instant, her startled laughter rang out as he swung her up into his arms and headed toward the bedroom.

WARM SATIN caressed the length of Mark's body as he floated in the pulsing aftermath of their loving. Sheri lay half on top of him in a graceful sprawl, her legs entwined with his. The uneven cadence of her breathing tickled the hair on his chest and her eyes were closed in utter exhaustion. The last fiery rays of the setting sun poured through the window, turning the sheets and their naked bodies to molten gold—a color similar to the fireball that had exploded behind his tightly closed eyelids only moments before.

He drew a shaky breath and smiled. That last one had been a real earth mover. And yet there had been poignant tenderness, too, an unspoken healing of the wounds they'd inflicted upon each other.

I love you, beautiful dancer, he thought, his heartbeat picking up again. As if she'd heard him speak the words, she raised her head and gave him a smile that warmed him to the very core of his being.

"Wow, that was more than I expected," she murmured.

Mark felt a twist of unease. Was she referring to the sex or what he'd been thinking? After all that mindreading talk earlier, he wasn't sure he'd like her answer, so he decided not to ask for clarification. Instead he pulled her up until her lovely breasts were pressing softly against his chest and her mouth was hovering within kissing range.

"More than you expected?" he groused gently. "How can you say that after what happened the first time we made love? When I finally staggered home that night, I felt as if I'd experienced a nuclear explosion at ground zero." He gave her a teasing scowl. "Did you think I wouldn't be able to pull it off again?"

She gave him a long significant look, then said, "I never had any doubts about *that*. And this time was even better."

"Even better, huh?" He smiled, and began to stroke the creamy curve of her bottom. And when he felt the moist tip of her tongue flick teasingly along the line of his upper lip, he forgot everything except the incredible beauty of her taste and the satiny softness of her skin.

SHERI AWOKE with a start early the next morning, and a little rush of panic accosted her heart when she realized the other side of the bed was empty. Last night Mark had promised they'd share breakfast. Had he changed his mind and left without even saying goodbye? Or, worse yet, had daylight brought a cold flash of reason, making him reconsider his grand promises to accept her, foibles and all?

A small thump and the sound of running water came from the direction of the kitchen, and relief flooded her soul. He hadn't left. Hastily pulling on Mark's discarded shirt, she headed toward the sound.

She found him making coffee, jeans riding low on his hips. His tanned back gleamed golden in the pale morning light, and his platinum-streaked hair was attractively tousled. For a moment she simply stood there, drinking in his masculine perfection, savoring the poignancy of her love for him. Then, silent as a cat, she moved up behind him and slid her arms around his waist. "Don't move, buster. I've got you covered," she announced gruffly.

His body tensed for an instant, then relaxed. "Oh yeah? What do you intend to do now?"

"Frisk you." She began a leisurely exploration of the taut hollows in his hips and the bunched muscles behind. Mark's breathing quickened, and she felt him tense as she proceeded down the sinewy length of his legs and back up again. But his silent control cracked when she slowly stroked the front of his half-open fly.

Inhaling sharply he said, "I hate to tell you this, but I never carry my gun there."

"Hmm, feels like a concealed weapon to me." Soft laughter rippled in her voice as she reached inside the denim opening and found the solid heat of his tumescence. Just the feel of his renewed desire sent a white-hot flash of need through her. "Mark, I want you," she whispered, drawing him toward a kitchen chair and urging him to sit. "Right now."

Eyes glinting, he eased off his jeans and drew her onto his lap, making her spread her legs until she was nestled intimately against him.

"Yes, like that!" she cried, feeling his first thrilling probe.

But he pulled back with a gentle, "Wait, honey. I forgot one little detail."

Tamping down her impatience, she took the small packet he'd pulled from his jeans and said, "Allow me." By the time she'd finished the intimate task, Mark was gasping.

"Now, where were we?" she inquired with a little smirk.

"Right here." Mark's strong hands gripped her bottom, bringing her up and over him. With one swift thrust he buried himself deep inside her, and she uttered a hoarse cry of satisfaction. And then they were moving together, each driven by the same desperation, each striving to give and receive maximum pleasure. She felt Mark nuzzle his way inside the open front of the shirt she wore, then his warm avid mouth found her breast. Within moments the first starburst of sensation tore through her and she would have tumbled to the floor if Mark's arms hadn't been there to support her.

Afterward they remained like that, wrapped in each other's arms, and she felt his chest expand against her in a contented sigh.

"Could we just stay like this forever?" he asked, his words muffled by the tumbled waves of her hair.

Sheri chuckled and burrowed closer into his neck. "I wish! Unfortunately, duty calls for both of us."

"I hope that doesn't include tonight. I was going to ask you to join April and me for dinner and a movie. Much as I'd like to have you all to myself, I think you two should have some more time to get to know each other."

Sheri groaned unhappily. "I want that too, but I can't tonight. There's a jazz concert at the store." She sat up and gave him a hopeful smile. "You and April could come, if you like. The music is great and everyone is so friendly, I'll bet she loves it."

Mark's brow wrinkled doubtfully. "I've never cared for jazz. I'm more a country music fan."

She leaned forward until they were nose to nose and said, "Compromise, remember?" Then she fluttered her eyelashes and added, "And I'll be there."

A slow, intimate grin creased his lean face. "Maybe I should give jazz another try."

"I WAS RIGHT about April," Sheri announced to Mark that evening as she finished ringing up another sale. "She's having the time of her life."

Mark leaned against the front counter and watched as his daughter scurried around serving pastries and other snacks to the customers crowding Café Gourmet's festive interior. "She loves to help." He favored Sheri with a warm smile. "And I think she'd do just about anything for you. It's uncanny the way she took to you. The other women I dated . . ." He stopped, looking chagrined.

The other women, Sheri thought. None of whom managed to win your love. She felt a stab of uncertainty, but laughed lightly to cover it. "I know, she told me. Especially about the one who was fat on top." She glanced down at herself and quipped, "I have to admit, I felt a little insecure after I heard about that one."

"What's making you feel insecure?" Sean inquired, approaching with a tray of used paper cups and plates he'd just collected.

"Mark's buxom girlfriend."

Before Sean could comment, Mark had grabbed her hands and pulled her halfway over the counter. "You don't have anything to feel insecure about," he said gruffly. To prove his point, he kissed her long and hard.

A smattering of applause broke out around them when he released her, and she heard Sean say, "Nice comeback, Mark, but I think you should continue the demonstration in the back room."

"Right," Mark agreed, coming around the counter to guide her through the doorway. But he'd barely begun to take her into his arms when they were interrupted by one of Sheri's teenage waitresses.

"Sheri, it's him!" Annie announced excitedly, popping her head around the doorjamb. "Remember the creepy guy I told you about last week? Well, he was here again, staring at you through the window."

"What creepy guy?" Mark demanded, his body tensing.

Sheri gestured helplessly. "Remember I told you Annie thought this man was ogling me last Sunday night? Although I don't know how she could tell I was the object of his attention, given the number of people we had packed in here. Anyway, Sean looked around outside, and he didn't see anyone who fitted Annie's description...." Her voice faded as Mark abruptly released her and advanced upon a startled Annie.

"What did he look like?"

"B-big," Annie stammered. "And kinda weird looking. You know, like he wasn't too bright."

"Anything else?" Mark urged impatiently.

"Well...it was too dark for me to see what color his hair was." She frowned, concentrating. "Oh, yeah, he was wearing a denim jacket."

Mark sent Sheri a warning look. "Stay put. I'm going to have a look around."

When he returned a while later, he didn't look too happy.

"Any luck?" Sheri inquired, handing two steaming cups of espresso to Annie.

He shook his head. "I thought I saw someone duck into the alley down the street, but by the time I got there he was gone."

She reached to give his hand a squeeze before returning to her espresso machine. "Don't go looking for trouble. It was probably just some harmless old bum enjoying the music."

"What if it was the guy who's been calling you ever since he swiped your car?"

She scowled and shook her head. "I don't think so. He was pretty mad after he found out you'd come with me to that bar, and he hasn't called since."

"All the same, I want you to be extra careful. April and I will follow you home tonight, just to be on the safe side."

"That's not necessary—" she began, but he stopped her with a finger pressed to her lips.

"Compromise, remember?"

"Oh, all right. But I think you're worrying about nothing."

HALF A MILE AWAY, Denny stopped to rest behind a deserted store, his lungs aching, his heart battering his chest like a giant piston. Leaning against the rickety wooden door, he placed his hands upon his knees and breathed in great sobs.

The cop! She'd been with the cop and he'd kissed her! That single thought ran round and round his brain like a sharp-clawed hamster on an exercise wheel. After a bit his breathing slowed and his heart calmed down, but the pain remained.

He slid to a sitting position and rested his forehead on his upraised knees. *It's all your fault, too, Stupid, a taunting inner voice told him. You shouldn'ta blown your cool and told her she'd never get her car back. Maybe if you'd given her another chance and made sure she came alone...*

Denny shifted his shoulders irritably. He'd messed up once trying to plan something like that; no point in wondering if a second attempt would have been more successful. And yet he couldn't let go of the dream that had haunted him ever since he'd first seen her. A dream where she looked at him like he was a regular guy and even liked him. A dream where they went off someplace, just the two of them, so she couldn't compare him to other men. Like that cop.

Slowly he raised his head as the idea took root and grew. Alone. He had to get her alone somehow. He still had that little red car of hers. Maybe he should give it another try. She'd followed him once when she'd seen him driving it. He could get her to do it again. That way she wouldn't have time to call her cop friend. She'd be all alone with no one to help her....

"Except me," Denny said with a satisfied grunt. Anticipation spurred him into action and he got up and shambled off into the darkness, churning plans in his mind like a cement mixer.

9

SHERI KNEW her attention wasn't fully on her driving as she guided her brother's car through the Kensington area's afternoon traffic. Mark Sampson had occupied her thoughts for most of the past week. She smiled and touched the delicate gold bracelet he'd given her the day before. A tiny, exquisitely crafted carousel horse dangled from the fragile chain.

Her smile widened as she started to recall just how she had thanked him, but her awareness of her surroundings sharpened when she spotted the bright red paint job of the elegant sports car a block and a half ahead.

"There are probably dozens of red 450SLs in San Diego," she told herself firmly. But her foot pressed down harder on the gas pedal, and she began to gain on the other vehicle. She could scarcely believe her eyes when she got close enough to see the license plate. "That's my car! It's even the right license number this time." Instantly cautious, she deliberately slowed and allowed two cars to cut in between her and her quarry. She didn't want the other driver spotting her and racing off before she could do something to catch him.

"Now what?" she wondered aloud as the other car drove onto the freeway and headed toward the less attractive industrial section of the city. She had no intention of confronting the driver of the other car by herself, but she couldn't just let him get away, either.

Only one solution presented itself: follow discreetly until the other car stopped long enough for her to find a telephone and call Mark.

Employing the few tailing techniques she'd gleaned over the years from television and movies, she maintained a healthy distance from the little Mercedes, whose driver seemed unaware of her pursuit. After employing the old "nip in behind a parked car to wait out a red light" trick for the second time, she began congratulating herself. This should prove to Mark he didn't have to worry about her running off to do wild, irresponsible things.

She glanced a little nervously at the run-down buildings on both sides of the street. Okay, so it wasn't the best part of town, but she had daylight on her side and the presence of other human beings who worked in the area. Engrossed in imagining Mark's praise for her levelheaded plan, she almost missed the quick left turn the other car made into a narrow side street lined on either side with huge warehouses. Sheri slowed to a crawl and eased past for a quick glance, but she didn't see the Mercedes, only a faint mist of settling dust left by its passing. Strange, since the street appeared to be a dead end.

Sheri worried her lower lip with her teeth. Should she follow? A survey of the surrounding area revealed a wrecking yard a little farther down the main street, and a gas station displaying a public phone sign just beyond. She could call Mark from there, but what if that side street wasn't a dead end? What if there was another way out? Her car would be long gone by the time Mark arrived. Gritting her teeth, she put the VW into gear and decided to do a little reconnaissance. After all, the car doors were locked, and if she sensed any danger, she could simply stomp on the gas and drive away.

Loose gravel popped under the tires as she inched her way down the cramped alley. The giant doors of the warehouses were all closed, except for one toward the end, which gaped open to accommodate a huge, decrepit-looking dump truck. The front end had been smashed in and the oversize headlamps seemed to glare at her as she drove by. Seized by a strong feeling that she'd made a severe tactical error, Sheri accelerated to the end of the passageway. She'd been right, it was a dead end.

Her heart beginning to pound, she executed a three-point turn and headed back the way she'd come. But she had to slam on the brakes when, with an ugly roar, the engine of the dump truck came to life and the monstrous vehicle surged forward, blocking her way. Fighting an urge to scream, she watched as a figure that seemed as massive as the truck got out of the driver's seat and started toward her. Something about his wide homely face pricked her memory, but she was too frightened to pursue it.

He smiled, if that grimace could be called a smile, and waved at her, motioning for her to roll down her window. When she refused, he shrugged and turned away, fishing in the pocket of his denim jacket.

Denim jacket, Sheri's frantic mind repeated. Hadn't Annie said something about a big guy in a denim jacket? Oh, damn! Too late, she made the connection. Too late, she saw the odd tool in his hand. She jammed the gearshift into Reverse and tried to back up, but he had punched out the lock and yanked the door open before she could pick up any speed. A moot point anyway, she thought despairingly as huge hands pulled her out of the seat. Where could she have gone with the truck blocking her way?

Still she fought, screaming, kicking and scratching, landing as many blows as she could before he trapped her arms and clamped one ham-sized palm over her mouth and nose. Within moments, lack of oxygen had the world spinning away from under her feet, and as she felt herself slip helplessly into unconsciousness, she heard a voice, strangely familiar in its thick, halting cadence, mumble, "Sheri...Sheri, don't be scared. I'm gonna take good care of you."

THE TELEPHONE RANG in Mark's kitchen, interrupting his perusal of the refrigerator's discouraging contents.

"Mark, this is Sean O'Reilly. I wondered if you knew where Sheri is. No one's seen or heard from her since she left to run some errands, and she should have been back here by now."

"I haven't spoken to her since this morning." He examined a container with suspiciously green contents and tossed it into the trash. "Maybe she got involved in something and forgot the time."

"My sister may have some faults, but irresponsibility isn't one of them," Sean responded firmly. "Especially when it comes to business. Our grandmother hammered that lesson into her the hard way."

Mark winced. It appeared Sheri wasn't the only O'Reilly sensitive on the subject of responsibility. "I wasn't implying a lack of responsibility. Anyone can forget the time occasionally. Have you contacted any of her friends?"

"Not yet. I figured you'd be the most logical one to start with." Sean paused and added meaningfully, "Considering all the time you've spent together lately."

"If that's a subtle probe into my intentions, I can assure you they're honorable," Mark said, then let the refrigerator door swing shut as the impact of his last words sank in. Honorable intentions, as in long-term commitment and love? Yeah, that about covered the way he was feeling lately. The knowledge rocked him pleasantly.

Sean cleared his throat nervously. "I didn't mean to sound like an overprotective brother. But I care very deeply about her. I guess that's why I'm so worried about her not returning on time. She only had a few errands right here in the area." He drew a quick breath. "This may sound crazy to you, but all afternoon I've had the strongest feeling that something is very wrong."

A tiny frisson of alarm went through Mark, but he forced himself to remain calm. "All right then, what we need is a plan. Why don't you call some of her friends and I'll do some checking from here." He kindly refrained from adding he would be contacting headquarters to get the current accident reports. He consulted the clock on the wall. "If either of us hears anything we'll call the other immediately. If not, let's check in at seven, that's an hour and a half from now."

By seven o'clock that evening, Mark had begun to feel as frantic as Sean sounded when he called back.

"None of her friends have seen or heard from her, nor have any of her neighbors. Have you had any luck?"

"No, nothing." Mark frowned and reached back to massage the headache that had begun to pound. "I even checked the hospitals." Unfortunately, April had overheard him at it and had demanded to know what was going on. He'd tried to minimize the situation, but he had a sinking feeling she'd seen right through his vague explanations. Since then she'd been ensconced on the couch with a pile of her stuffed animals, a sure sign that she was upset.

"What do we do now?" Sean asked, barely contained emotion weighing each word.

"You should stay near the phone, in case she tries to call you. I'm going down to headquarters and talk to the night shift before they head out. It can't hurt to have the patrol cars keep an eye out for your VW. That is what she was driving, isn't it?"

"Yes. And there's something else I think you should know...." Sean cleared his throat again. "Remember what I said about sensing something was wrong? Well, there's more to it than that. When Sheri and I were kids, we used to be...uh, sensitive to each other. It happens sometimes with twins."

Mark felt a queer twisting sensation in the pit of his stomach. "Are you talking about feelings or mental telepathy?"

"Either...no, both," Sean responded, sounding uncomfortable. "I know it sounds crazy, but we really did communicate until I deliberately put an end to it years ago. Since then there hasn't been any connection at all, but today I felt something again. Not really a message, like we used to send back and forth, more like a disconnected image. I keep seeing a wrecking yard, but I can't imagine what that has to do with Sheri."

A chill ran up Mark's spine. Regardless of his impulse to scoff at the idea of thought transference, a possible link between Sheri and wrecking yards occurred to him immediately. Stolen cars frequently ended up in wrecking yards, and people who stole cars occasionally worked in such places. And one car thief in particular had recently shown an unhealthy interest in Sheri. What if he had . . . ? Mark muttered an uncustomarily vile oath.

"Was that a commentary on my sanity?" Sean quipped.

"No, but I'm hoping that your intuition or whatever you call it is wrong this time." When Sean demanded to know what he meant, he gave a terse recap of the anonymous phone calls Sheri had received and the fateful rendezvous in the Chula Vista bar.

Sean's curse exceeded Mark's in intensity and volume. "Why didn't she tell me any of that? No, you don't have to say it, I know. Ever since I moved back to San Diego she's had this annoying notion that she has to protect me." He made a short sound of disgust. "I'll have to do something about correcting that misconception the next time I see her."

"Let's hope that happens soon," Mark added fervently. "If the night shift doesn't turn anything up tonight, tomorrow morning I'm going to start a systematic search of every wrecking yard in the county."

"Count me in." Sean's deep voice wavered a little as he added, "We have to find her, Mark. If anything happened to her it would be like losing a piece of myself."

"I know the feeling."

RANK DARKNESS embraced Sheri in the storage room where she lay bound and gagged. The acrid stench of dirty oil and rusting metal made it necessary for her to fight a constant swirling nausea. She couldn't afford to get sick with her mouth blocked as it was. How long had she been here? Hours? Days?

She had a vague memory of regaining consciousness in time to feel the gag being stuffed into her mouth. Then there had been a sickening sweet odor coming from a cloth held over her nose and after that blackness. When she'd come to the second time, she'd been hanging over the massive shoulder of her captor like a sack of potatoes. She'd gotten an upside-down view of a filthy office and beyond it the jumble of a wrecking yard—neither showing any sign of life— before she'd been deposited in the windowless room where she now lay.

Shifting gingerly, she felt around behind her until her fingers encountered something cold and hard. Metal. A tool of some kind. And beyond that another. Maybe if she found one with a sharp edge . . .

The sound of approaching voices made her freeze.

"I'm tellin' ya, Luther. It ain't in the back room." It was the voice of the man who'd captured her. The voice of the man who'd been phoning her.

"If you don't mind I'll just look for myself," a second male voice snapped. "I remember the last time I sent you to find something."

Sheri heard the grate of the doorknob being turned and then the door swung open. A shaft of bright light poured into the room, partially blinding her. Instinct made her keep her eyelids lowered, feigning unconsciousness, but through her lashes she could make out two shapes, one massive, the other strikingly short.

"Cripes! There's a broad in here. You big idiot, that's why you didn't want me looking around, isn't it? What's she doing there?"

"Uh, she followed me."

Sheri covertly focused her gradually adjusting vision on the smaller man. He had the tough stringy build of a featherweight fighter, and beneath thinning black hair his eyes were as cold and calculating as a vulture's.

"Dogs follow you home, Denny. Women don't. Especially one who looks like her." He indicated Sheri with a jerk of his head.

Carefully she switched her gaze to the big one called Denny. "This one did," he insisted, belligerence tightening his moonish face.

"I'll give you two seconds to tell me why." The one called Luther glowered threateningly, and to Sheri's amazement, the larger man cringed.

"The little red Mercedes . . . it's hers. I let her see me driving it, and she followed me here easy as anything. I...I wasn't gonna leave her here for good. I got a safe place where I can keep her out by the desert."

Sheri's blood ran cold. Keep her? The man was insane!

Apparently Luther held the same opinion. "Are you crazy? Stealing cars is one thing, but kidnapping is quite another. I'm running fifty or more hot cars through here a month, and you just put the whole operation at risk by snatching that broad. Kidnapping brings out the cops in swarms, you moron."

Realization swept over Sheri, sinking her spirits even deeper. Not only was her abductor insane, it sounded like he was part of a major auto-theft ring. One to which she had now become a liability.

"We've got to get her out of here," Luther went on. "But first I want you to get rid of that damned red car. You left it parked where anyone could see it. Run it over to the scrap yard and put it through the crusher." Sheri saw him give her a sour look. "Is she tied securely? I'm supposed to meet with a guy about a car in a few minutes, and I don't want her getting loose while you're gone. She'd have the cops down on our heads before you could spit."

"She's not goin' anywhere. I gave her something to knock her out," Denny said sullenly. "And I know how to tie good knots."

Luther snorted sarcastically. "Just what I need, a Boy Scout." He pulled the door shut, but she heard him add, "Wait for me at the other yard. I'll decide what to do with the broad when we get back here."

For a few seconds, right after the darkness enveloped her once more, panic got a stranglehold on Sheri's senses. She could think of only one way for them to ensure her silence. . . . No! She couldn't allow herself to dwell on that. She needed to concentrate on getting out of here. And the first order of business would be finding a way to rid herself of the heavy rope binding her wrists and ankles. Surely there must be something sharp in the mess of junk surrounding her.

Precious minutes ticked past; she squirmed around in the dark, frantically groping with bound hands, before giving up with a muffled cry of anguish. It might take hours to find a suitable cutting edge without benefit of sight, and she didn't have that kind of time. Flexing her hands in frustration, she felt the rope stretch infinitesimally, and a faded childhood memory filtered into her mind.

Once, when the circus train had been stalled in the middle of nowhere by a washed-out railroad bridge, she and Sean had spent an entire day learning escape tricks from old Freddie, better known as The Amazing Disappearing Man—No Bond Can Hold Him!

You can do it, she told herself, cautiously beginning the contract-and-relax sequence she'd learned so
long ago. Thank heaven, she'd kept her hands fairly
limber with the sinuous movements of belly dancing.
Minutes ticked past—or was it hours? Who could tell
in this pitch-dark, timeless void? Only one certainty
hammered in her brain: her time was running out.

By the time she'd worked her wrist bone free, perspiration was trickling down into her stinging eyes,
and her breathing sounded like that of a marathon
runner. With a strangled shout of triumph, she yanked
her hand the rest of the way out. She felt the bracelet
on her wrist snap and fall away, but didn't allow herself to give it a second thought as she tore at the binding that held her gag in place. Sheri only paused for a
few gasping breaths before attacking the ropes holding her ankles. That accomplished, she got up and
unsteadily felt her way to the door. It wasn't locked.

Easing the door open, she peered into the office and
discovered day had slipped away into night during her
captivity. Outside the yard was dark, except for twin
circles of light coming from a pair of floodlights
mounted on the front of the building. Better yet, the
place appeared deserted. Gathering her courage, she
slipped through the office and out the front door.

Mountains of ruined cars loomed all around, but a
dirt lane ran through the wreckage toward the gate of
a high chain-link fence. The gate appeared to be
locked, but beyond that she could see a street and far-

ther on a gas station—the same one she'd seen just before she'd driven into Denny's trap. Her heart pounding, she ran for the gate and began to climb, not caring that the metal links bit cruelly into her hands as she pulled herself upward.

Halfway to the top, she glanced down the street and saw the headlights of an approaching vehicle. "No," she breathed in anguish. "Please don't let it be . . ."

The truck accelerated as it drew nearer, and she knew her plea had gone unheeded. She scrambled back down and began to run toward the stacks of junked cars. Behind her she heard a roar of fury from Luther and an indistinct response from Denny as they struggled to unlock the gate. A grating sound announced their success, just as she ducked around a battered old Ford. From that point on it was only a matter of time until they found her, although she doggedly avoided capture for ten wearying minutes.

Denny finally cornered her by the rear fence, and as they faced each other breathlessly, his heavy features sagged with fatigue and what might have been regret. "Ya shouldn'ta run, Sheri," he said dully. "Now Luther won't never let you go."

He dragged her back to the office where Luther waited, his eyes burning with a hellish light. "That cinches it," he informed Denny coldly. "We have to dispose of her. Permanently. And I know just the way to do it."

FROM THE DRIVER'S SEAT of his Bronco, Mark surveyed the jumbled mess of the wrecking yard—his fourth that morning—and had to fight a crushing wave of despair. He had every man he could spare checking yards all over the county, but no sign of Sheri had been found so far.

Maybe he shouldn't have listened to Sean's crazy hunch. He glanced at Sheri's brother, who was sitting in the passenger seat, craning his neck to gaze about him. Something about the avid look in his deep hazel eyes and the russet highlights of his hair reminded Mark so sharply of Sheri, he felt as if a knife had been thrust into his heart. Maybe this was all a waste of time, but he was willing to try anything to get her back.

"Guess we'd better start checking," he said. "You remember the drill. If you see something suspicious, signal me."

They got out and Sean started walking around, while Mark went into the office and spoke to the man behind the counter, a morose-looking Goliath in a denim jacket and a baseball cap that had Denny the Dude embroidered on the visor.

Mark offered him an easy smile. "My buddy and I are scouting for some oddball parts for an old car we're fixing up. We'll let you know if we find anything we want." The counterman uttered a noncommittal grunt in response, but his eyes shifted away a little too fast.

The small sign didn't escape Mark, nor did the niggling feeling in the back of his mind—a strange conviction that he knew the guy from somewhere. He sauntered into the yard and began looking around, keenly aware that the guy behind the counter had abandoned his post to watch from the door of the office.

A short while later Sean appeared, looking agitated. "No sign of her," he said in response to Mark's inquiring glance. "But she's been here or somewhere nearby, I'm certain of it. I want to take a look around inside the building. Can you distract that big thug over there long enough for me to do it?"

Mark shook his head, his expression grim. "No, if anyone does any searching inside it will be me. I never thought I'd hear myself say this, but I've got a funny feeling about the place, too." He pulled a wry face. "I'd rather not wait for a search warrant, so just for the record, you didn't see me do this. More importantly, make sure that Denny the Dude over there doesn't catch me at it."

Sean smiled tightly. "I'll make it a big distraction." He disappeared from sight and a few minutes later a gigantic crash came from the back of the yard, followed by an agonized howl. The counterman looked alarmed and loped off in the direction of the sound, and as Mark slipped into the building, he uttered a fervent prayer that Sean was only acting.

A swift search of the office yielded nothing to indicate Sheri had been there, and Mark ground his teeth in frustration as he moved toward the cramped hallway beyond, which had two doors. The first led to a filthy bathroom, the second to an equally disgusting storeroom.

As he looked at the piles of discarded auto parts, illuminated by the light from the hall, his heart sank. No sign of Sheri. Yet the uneasy feeling he'd had earlier intensified as he stood there. He stepped into the room and poked around in the litter. Nothing.

Sheri, love, where are you? He turned to go, then hesitated, his gaze catching on an odd glint amid the grimy pieces of metal. When he bent to investigate, his heart began to beat a little faster. Gold. It was a gold chain. Oh, sweet heaven, it was the bracelet he'd given her two days before! There could be no mistake, not with that little carousel horse on it.

He felt adrenaline begin to pour into his system and with it a simmering rage. Sheri had been here, and knowing that made several other pieces of the puzzle click into place for him. Hadn't one of Sheri's employees noticed a big guy in a denim jacket hanging around and watching Sheri? And the night they'd gone to that bar in Chula Vista, there'd been a hulking type in a denim jacket at the end of the bar, who'd practically had his nose in his beer the whole time. Maybe to avoid having his face seen? Oh yes, the pieces were starting to come together, and Mark had a hunch Denny was involved right up to his bullish neck.

He stepped back into the office just as Denny came charging in, his face twisted in a scowl. "You ain't supposed to be in there."

Mark shrugged and pulled out his police revolver. "Maybe not, but neither is the bracelet I just found on the floor." With his free hand he flipped out his ID badge. "I'm Sergeant Sampson, San Diego police, and I'd appreciate it if you didn't move." Mark flicked his eyes to the door.

"Glad to see you survived, Sean. I hit pay dirt in the back room. Sheri was here, just as you suspected. We're going to need a search warrant and some backup, but first Denny the Dude here is going to tell us what he's done with her."

Denny's face grew sullen. "I don't know nothin' and I don't squeal to cops."

Mark tightened his grip on the gun and brought it up to a firing position. "I suggest you reconsider. I think you know a great deal, and unless you start talking fast, I may forget I'm a cop."

10

MARK HELD the gun steady, but inside his whole being screamed for action as he waited for Denny's answer. Each passing moment could be crucial to Sheri's safety. If it wasn't already too late.

He rejected the thought with a jerk of his head and narrowed his eyes at his prisoner.

"I didn't do nothin'," Denny insisted.

"You're the one who stole her car, aren't you?" It was a guess, but Mark figured he had nothing to lose. "And then you started harassing her by telephone. Add to that a possible kidnapping charge and you're in big trouble, Denny. But even that is minimal compared to the kind of time you'll get if any harm has come to Miss O'Reilly."

To Mark's amazement, Denny looked outraged and burst out with, "I never woulda hurt her. That was Luther's idea. I just wanted to keep her with me." His coarse features seemed to droop with defeat. "I figured she might like me if I was the only guy around."

The idea of Sheri being at the mercy of a man like Denny was enough to fill Mark with a killing rage, but he was careful not to show it. And when Sean made a low, threatening sound, Mark sent him a quelling look. Denny's misguided attachment to Sheri might prove useful if it was played on correctly.

Mark allowed his gun hand to relax a little. "I can see why you'd want her to yourself," he said sympathetically. "She's very beautiful, isn't she? Too beautiful to let a guy like Luther do anything to her."

Denny brought a hamlike fist down onto the counter in a thundering crash. "I tried to talk him outa it. He just wouldn't listen. He never listens to me."

"He'll listen to me, Denny," Mark said with quiet urgency. "Just tell me where he's taken her."

Shaking his head in defeat, Denny mumbled, "Won't do no good. Luther don't listen to no one."

"Let me try," Mark implored, fighting an urge to throttle the man. "For Sheri's sake."

An odd light appeared in Denny's deep-set eyes. "She shouldn't havta die. You gotta stop him. He took her to the scrap yard in National City."

"The address?" Mark demanded, already dialing police headquarters from the telephone on the counter. Within minutes he'd relayed the address Denny had given him and had ordered a patrol unit to be sent there, in addition to a backup unit to pick up Denny.

The wait for the backup's arrival seemed interminable to Mark and Sean, although it couldn't have been more than ten minutes before they were on their way. As the Bronco tore out of the driveway, spewing dust, Sean braced himself and said tersely, "I just pray to God we're not too late."

Mark responded without taking his eyes off the road. "I've been doing that since the first time you called me yesterday."

AS SHERI STRAINED for what must have been the thousandth time against the tight bindings that held her, and she found herself expending an equal amount of inner energy fighting black despair. It had begun that morning, when Luther hadn't bothered to offer her breakfast. One didn't need a degree in psychology to understand the sinister implication of his omission, although she'd struggled hard to avoid slipping into despondency.

As long as there was fight left in her there was hope, she kept telling herself, lying in the darkness of yet another storage room. She'd managed to survive the night, hadn't she? That had to be a small miracle, considering Luther's temper when they'd arrived at his scrap metal yard, only to discover the crushing machine had broken down in the middle of compacting her Mercedes. Even the dark horror of what he'd obviously planned for her hadn't dimmed her optimism over that providential reprieve.

Until now, she admitted, relaxing to give her aching, fatigue-racked muscles a rest. She'd fought against her bonds off and on all night long, using the times in between to send up fervent little prayers, promising to reform her adventuresome ways if given another chance. And longer, more eloquent pleas regarding her future with Mark.

"Please, get me out of this," she whispered yet again against the rough fabric of her gag. *I haven't even told him how much I love him*. That thought hurt her more than the ravaged flesh on her wrists and ankles.

The thud of approaching footsteps caught her attention, and a moment later the door was unlocked and thrust open. "Cover her with this blanket and put her in the trunk of that green '58 Buick," Luther ordered, stepping into the room.

Blinking in the sudden stream of sunlight, Sheri barely had time to make out the shape of another man before coarse fabric encompassed her. Rough hands hauled her aching body up and onto a hard shoulder, and she couldn't stop a strangled cry of pain.

A jostling ride followed, then she was being lowered into the close confines of a car's trunk. The lid slammed shut before she could wrestle her head out of the blanket, so her eyes encountered only darkness once she'd shaken off the stifling fabric.

She heard Luther's voice just outside saying, "This one's next in the crusher, as soon as Jonas gets the damned thing running."

As if in answer, Sheri heard the sound of a big diesel engine starting up, then choking into silence. She closed her lips tight, holding in a scream that seemed to ring in her ears for an eternity. Then she realized the shrill noise was coming from outside.

Sweet heaven! Was that a police siren?

It was! The sound drew nearer and stopped, and she heard Luther launch into a string of obscenities. "Cops! Damn it, they couldn't be on to the broad being here, not if Denny told the truth about her not having time to contact anyone. I'll see what they want," he snarled to the other man. "You go tell Jonas to get the lead out. Once that car's been smashed, there won't be any incriminating evidence."

Sheri's heart began to thud painfully in her chest. Luther was right, there wasn't any way the police could know she was here. Still, she couldn't prevent a desperate little flicker of hope. Minutes slogged by, then more minutes without any sound except the wild beating of her pulse to fill the stuffy interior of the trunk.

Her hope slowly dimmed and had nearly died when another sound caught her attention. At first she thought she'd imagined it, like a dying man sees an oasis in the desert. But then it came again—the drawl of Mark's voice—and she knew she wasn't dreaming, even though he wasn't near enough for her to make out what he was saying.

Joy shot through her like a comet, lighting her very soul, but right on its heels came a new panic. The distinctive roar of a diesel engine suddenly drowned all other sound, and it was soon joined by the racket of another, similar engine nearby.

Something smashed into the car that held her, jostling her cruelly, and she heard the tinkle of breaking glass and the screech of metal upon metal. The car seemed to lurch upward.

The explanation came with sickening speed. They were loading the car into the crusher. And with the racket outside, Mark wouldn't be able to hear her, even if she had some way to signal him. The combined sound from the engines made it difficult for her even to hear her own thoughts.

Thoughts! The idea sprang from sheer desperation. She'd been able to read Mark's thoughts, and once upon a time Sean had been able to read hers. Maybe she could reach Mark that way.

Focusing every ounce of her energy, she began to send a silent message—again and again. *Mark . . . Mark, I'm in the trunk of a green '58 Buick. Near the crusher. The green Buick, Mark. Please hear me. . . .*

MARK HEARD the distant growl of two large engines firing up and tried to contain his teeth-grinding impatience as he scanned the vast jumble of Luther Smizer's scrap-metal yard. Sheri was out there somewhere. He could almost feel her presence. And he had the unnerving idea that her time was about to run out.

He eyed Luther contemptuously. The man reminded him of a sewer rat, mean and clever and totally amoral. Questioning him had been futile—he simply refused to answer without having an attorney present.

A thick pall of impending doom pressed in upon Mark, prompting him to snarl, "Last chance, Mr. Smizer. Where is she?" Luther just smirked and refused to answer.

Barely able to contain his fury, Mark turned to the two officers who'd arrived on the scene before him. "Turner, keep an eye on this guy. Burke, you, Sean and I will spread out and start combing the grounds. Considering the threat to Sheri's life, I'm not going to wait for Lou to arrive with the search warrant." They spread out, heading in three different directions.

As Mark peered into the empty shells of junked cars and behind piles of assorted metal castoffs, a silent litany filled his mind. *Sheri, love, where are you? Please, God, let her be all right.*

The roar of the engines sounded nearer, and he jogged around a stack of compacted cars to find its source. He arrived just in time to see an old green Buick being swung up on the prongs of a forklift toward the waiting jaws of a crushing machine.

For a moment he watched, fascinated. Then a terrifying revelation welled up and exploded inside his mind. Sheri was in the trunk of that car! He didn't stop to question how or why he knew, he just acted. With a vicious cry he raced forward and jumped up beside the man operating the forklift, catching him just as he was about to release his cargo to its fate.

"Freeze!" Mark shouted, displaying his revolver in case his voice hadn't carried over the din. The startled man did as he was told, and when Mark ordered him to lower the car to the ground—gently—he complied and killed the engine. A motion from Mark's gun prompted the operator of the crusher to turn his machine off also.

In the ensuing silence Mark shouted again, this time for Burke and Sean to join him. They arrived at a run, as Mark turned the key that had been left in the lock of the doomed car's trunk. When the trunk lid swung up, a choked cry escaped him. "Sheri, sweetheart, are you all right?"

Squeezing her light-starved eyes tightly shut against the sudden brightness of day, Sheri heard Mark's voice and felt the gentle touch of his strong hands dispatching her bindings. Once free, she scrambled up and reached for him half blindly and shuddered in relief when she felt the hard security of his arms close around her. In the distance she heard the wail of more approaching sirens, and from somewhere nearby she heard her brother's voice.

"The bastards! They were actually going to—" He stopped, apparently too upset to go on.

"Mark, Mark," she repeated, then emotion-choked words tumbled out of her in a torrent. "I'm so sorry. I shouldn't have followed—but he had my car. Denny, the big one . . . and he's part of a big auto-theft ring . . . and Luther said they had to get rid of me, because I'd ruin everything."

She reared her head back to look at Mark and sudden tears stung her eyelids. "Oh, Mark, I was so afraid you wouldn't hear me, but you did, didn't you? You heard my thoughts. If you hadn't, I'd still be in that trunk. . . ." Her voice broke, and she looked toward the waiting maw of the crushing machine.

"Shh, don't think about it right now," he crooned, rocking her lightly. "You can tell me all about it later. Let's get you out of here." Can you put your arms around my neck? If you're not seriously injured, I'm going to carry you back to the entrance. I think I just heard the rest of our team arrive."

He lifted her tenderly and turned toward the other officer who was holding Luther's employees at gunpoint. "I'll send someone to give you a hand." He swung around and addressed Sheri's brother, who looked ready to tear into the two captives at the slightest provocation. "Sean, why don't you run ahead and tell the other officers they'd better restrain Mr. Smizer and any of his employees they find wandering around? I think we're on to something big here."

For Sheri, the rest of that day slipped by under the bewildering haze of her exhaustion. Looking back later, she could remember certain fragmented pieces, like the emergency-room doctor who'd bandaged her wrists and ankles and recommended bed rest for the aftereffects of shock. And then there had been Mark's mercifully brief interrogation, capped by a teary reunion with April, who had resolutely volunteered to stay and help Sean watch over his sister when Mark was forced to return to the ongoing investigation of Luther Smizer.

After a light meal, prepared by Sean and April, Sheri finally succumbed to the effects of her harrowing ordeal and fell into a deep sleep. She didn't wake until late that evening, when she came to with a start that jiggled the water bed's mattress. The near darkness of the room brought a spasm of panic to her throat until she saw the Minnie Mouse night-light someone had thoughtfully placed in an outlet by the bed. April's doing, no doubt.

Sheri smiled, recalling the little girl's fierce hug of greeting. How quickly they'd become attached to each other! And how devastating it would have been for the child if things hadn't turned out all right. Her smile faded. Hadn't that been one of the reasons for Mark's hesitation over becoming involved with her? That she would someday give in to her quixotic urges and desert him and April, just as his first wife had? By chasing after Denny, she'd nearly proved him tragically right.

A soft rap on the bedroom door caught her attention, and her heart jumped a little as she called, "Come in." But her hopes dimmed when Sean, not Mark, entered.

"Hey, sleepyhead," he said softly. "I hope I didn't wake you."

She scooted up to a sitting position, switched on the bedside lamp and tried to smooth the wrinkles out of the red satin chemise she'd put on before going to bed. Realizing the futility of her attempts, she pulled the sheet up to her chest and propped a pillow behind her. "I wasn't sleeping, just lying here worrying."

Sean moved to sit on the edge of the bed, his handsome features warming with a smile. But she saw his smile fade a little when he reached for her hand and saw the white bandages circling her wrists. "You don't have to worry anymore. You're safe now. Mark will see to that."

Sheri shook her head sorrowfully. "It's Mark I'm worrying about. I'm not so sure he'll ever be able to forget the horrible risk I took. I tried to apologize to him on the way to the hospital and again on the way back here, but he just kept putting me off, saying we'd discuss it later." She looked at the clock radio on the bed table. "It's nearly ten-thirty. Why didn't he come by to see me when he got off work?"

"He did," Sean replied calmly. "But you were dead to the world, and he had to take April home and get her settled for the night. He said he'd be back later."

"Probably didn't want April to witness our final farewell," Sheri deduced morosely. She drew her knees up and propped her forehead against them.

"That's crazy." Sean's voice sounded gruff, but his hand smoothed over her hair with the utmost gentleness. "He's in love with you, Sis. And I don't think anything you've done can change that. In fact, I'm so sure he's going to be around to take care of you, I've decided it's safe for me to move on."

Sheri's head came up in astonishment. "Move on? What are you talking about?"

Sean lifted one shoulder dismissively. "I'm feeling restless. Miming's been great, but I think I'd like to try something else—maybe see a little of the world while I'm at it."

Her worries about Mark momentarily forgotten, Sheri groaned and ran her hands through her tousled hair. "Now you sound like our father. I hope you're not going to spend your life wandering aimlessly, like he did." She grabbed his shoulder and faced him earnestly. "I know you won't like hearing it, but you're too intelligent for that. Your knowledge and ability could do so much good in this world, if only you'd settle down and use it." She might have gone on from there, but the disparaging look on Sean's face stopped her.

He studied her for a long moment, then grinned and reached to tweak her nose. "I haven't heard a sermon like that from you since we were twelve. Do you intend to go on? Or shall I pass the offering plate?"

She laughed and ruffled his thick hair. "All right, maybe it was a little preachy, but I'm concerned about what you plan to do. And if you're honest with yourself, you'll admit you haven't been living up to your potential lately."

"Believe it or not, I came to that realization myself a while back. And I intend to let you know what my plans are as soon as they're finalized, which they aren't. I wanted to make sure you were going to be all right before I went ahead with them."

Her mouth dropped open in astonishment. "*You* were concerned about *me?* But I'm the one who's settled. I have a business and a home—"

"And no one to share it with, until now," he interrupted gently. "Besides, after some of the wild adventures you've had lately, I figured you needed someone to look after you."

Indignation replaced bemusement. "I'm perfectly capable of taking care—'" She broke off, distracted, when the front doorbell chimed. Could it be Mark?

Sean got up and started toward the door. "That's probably the guy I had in mind for the job." He paused and looked back. "You do want to see him, don't you?"

Renewed panic skipped like a gremlin in her heart, but she drew a deep breath and nodded. "Yes. Good or bad, I'd rather have it over."

Sean shook his head. "Quit anticipating trouble. Everything will be fine."

She tried to smile. "Thanks. But even if it isn't, I don't want you to feel you have to stay. You need to pursue your own dreams, and I love you too much to ever stand in your way."

His eyes looked misty for a moment, then he simply said, "I know. I feel the same way about you," and closed the door.

She heard his steps moving down the hallway, the distinctive creak of the front door being opened and the low murmur of male voices before the door closed again. Then the thud of slow footsteps started back down the hall. Sean's or Mark's? She waited with her heart in her throat.

The door swung open and she saw Mark's lean frame silhouetted by the hall light. Happiness fluttered to life inside her like a million shimmering fairy wings, but she held it in check.

"Hello, love," he said, his deep voice gritty with fatigue. "I looked in on you earlier when I picked up April, but you were sleeping so peacefully, I didn't have the heart to wake you."

Even in the soft glow of the bedside lamp she could see the worry lines etched on his face. The variegated blond of his hair lay in grooved disarray, as if he'd been combing it with his fingers, and his striking blue eyes were bloodshot.

"I wouldn't have minded," she assured him softly. "You look so tired. Why don't you come sit down?" She patted a spot on the satiny sheets.

"I am bushed." He crossed the room and lowered himself cautiously to sit on the edge of the bed. "This has been the longest two days of my life. First not knowing where you were, then nearly losing you because of that monster, Luther...." He shook his head. "I hope I never have to go through that again."

Sheri's heart sank. "Does that mean you've come to say goodbye?"

He stopped in the act of reaching for her hand and gave her a startled look. "Goodbye? What do you mean?"

She shrugged, then tugged up the drooping strap of her chemise. "I thought maybe this last adventure of mine might have made you realize I'm too big a risk to have around." Her resolve grew. "Although I have to tell you, I've decided to make some major changes in my life-style."

"Not too major, I hope." He smiled slightly and lifted his hand to cup her cheek. "I happen to like you as you are, and so does my daughter."

"That may be," she agreed reluctantly, "but I couldn't bear the thought of putting you through anything like this again. I care too much for both of you. From now on I'm going to look—twice!—before I leap."

Mark chuckled and ran a fingertip down the slope of her shoulder. "I'm glad to hear that, because I've discovered I can't bear the thought of living without you." He took her hand, lacing their fingers together. Her heart began to trip along in double time.

"I need you in my life, Sheri. And since that includes cohabiting with me and my impressionable young daughter, I guess you'll have to marry me." He brought their joined hands to his mouth and gave her a piercing look. "Will you?"

Overwhelmed with joy, she took a small gasping breath and nodded. "Yes. And I promise I'll never, ever leave you."

Mark's features sagged a little with relief and then he was gently pulling her near, careful not to jar her bandaged wrists. "Thank heaven. I don't know how I would've explained to April if you'd said no."

Sheri laughed, nuzzling his neck, inhaling his clean scent. "She approves, then?"

"Heartily. And your brother told me when I arrived just now that I'd better hurry up and ask you, because he'll be moving on as soon as he sees us settled. He mentioned finding something more worthwhile to do with his life."

"So he told me. He claims he's been waiting for someone to take over the job of taking care of me." She pursed her mouth ruefully. "Although I suppose some people might think I need a keeper after the way I walked right into that trap Denny laid for me." She shuddered a little at the memory.

"You won't have to worry about him or Luther Smizer bothering you again for a long time," Mark said. He ran his hands soothingly over her shoulders, dislodging the straps of her nightgown. "We have enough evidence to get maximum sentences on the whole gang."

"So something good did come out of this whole thing." She inhaled sharply as he placed nibbling kisses down the slope of her shoulder.

"Yeah, you agreed to marry me, even though I didn't manage to find your car in time to save it from being destroyed."

"Mark, wait." She caught his face between her hands and made him look at her. "It doesn't matter to me about the car. The important thing is, you heard my messages and found me in time."

His eyes narrowed a bit. "Messages?" he inquired cautiously.

"Yes. The ones I sent to you when I was trapped in the trunk of that car. There wasn't any other way to signal you, so I used thought transference, just like I used to do with Sean when we were kids."

Mark looked pained. "Uh, honey, I didn't receive any messages."

"You must have," Sheri insisted. "How else could you have known where I was?"

"Simple deduction? Instinct? I don't know. . . ." He raked a hand through his hair. "I just can't buy all this paranormal stuff. Would it be so terrible if I didn't believe in it?"

Sheri started to argue, then caught herself. He looked so weary, she didn't have the heart to press such a minor point. "I guess you're right, it isn't that important." She grinned mischievously. "But don't think I'm not going to keep trying to convince you. Silently, of course."

"Of course," Mark said, smiling again. He lifted one of her bandaged wrists and kissed it softly. "Are you having much pain?"

"No. As a matter of fact, I feel pretty good at the moment. Can you stay for a while?"

"I can stay all night if you like. April's spending the night with a girlfriend, and Sean went home when I arrived. I know you're probably not up to making love right now, but if it's all right, I'd like to hold you."

"If you spend the night, you're going to have to do more than that," she retorted, skimming her mouth over his in a tantalizing caress. "We O'Reillys are a tough lot."

He slid one knuckle along the V neckline of her chemise and watched with satisfaction as the gleaming red satin slithered lower, revealing the full upper curve of her breasts. "That you are."

Together they eased down to the sleek comfort of the sheets and she drew him near, framing his face with her hands. Now was as good a time as any to start....

Looking straight into his eyes, she said without speaking, *Mark, I love you.*

At first he appeared startled then a little wary, and looked back at her for what seemed like ages. Then his eyes crinkled at the corners, and a reluctant grin deepened the charming grooves on either side of his mouth. "Okay, I'll agree to keep an open mind, but you're not going to convince me that easily."

Her delighted laughter bubbled between them as their mouths met in a deep, soul-stirring kiss. But then, as she felt herself slipping blissfully into the sweet forgetfulness of passion, an unexpected sensation stroked the depths of her mind and she heard the words as if he'd spoken them.

My beautiful dancer, I love you, too.

**THIS JULY, HARLEQUIN OFFERS YOU
THE PERFECT SUMMER READ!**

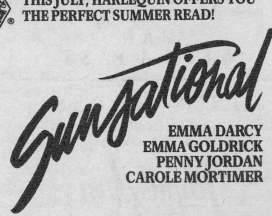

**EMMA DARCY
EMMA GOLDRICK
PENNY JORDAN
CAROLE MORTIMER**

From top authors of Harlequin Presents comes
HARLEQUIN SUNSATIONAL, a four-stories-in-one
book with 768 pages of romantic reading.

Written by such prolific Harlequin authors as Emma Darcy,
Emma Goldrick, Penny Jordan and Carole Mortimer,
HARLEQUIN SUNSATIONAL is the perfect summer
companion to take along to the beach, cottage, on your
dream destination or just for reading at home in the warm
sunshine!

Don't miss this unique reading opportunity.

Available wherever Harlequin books are sold.

HARLEQUIN
Romance®

**This August, travel to Spain
with the Harlequin Romance
FIRST CLASS title #3143,
SUMMER'S PRIDE
by Angela Wells.**

"There was a time when I would have given you everything I
possessed for the pleasure of taking you to my bed and loving
you...."

But since then, Merle's life had been turned upside down, and
now it was clear that cynical, handsome Rico de Montilla felt
only contempt toward her. So it was unfortunate that when she
returned to Spain circumstances forced her to seek his help.
How could she hope to convince him that she was not the
mercenary, unfeeling woman he believed her to be?

Back by Popular Demand

Janet Dailey
Americana

A romantic tour of America through fifty favorite Harlequin Presents, each set in a different state researched by Janet and her husband, Bill. A journey of a lifetime in one cherished collection.

In August, don't miss the exciting states featured in:

Title #13 — ILLINOIS
The Lyon's Share

#14 — INDIANA
The Indy Man

Available wherever
Harlequin books are sold.

Harlequin Superromance®

This August, don't miss Superromance #462—STARLIT PROMISE

STARLIT PROMISE is a deeply moving story of a woman coming to terms with her grief and gradually opening her heart to life and love.

Author Petra Holland sets the scene beautifully, never allowing her heroine to become mired in self-pity. It is a story that will touch your heart and leave you celebrating the strength of the human spirit.

Available wherever Harlequin books are sold.

STARLIT

 **Harlequin Books®**

GREAT NEWS...
HARLEQUIN UNVEILS NEW SHIPPING PLANS

For the convenience of customers, Harlequin has announced that Harlequin romances will now be available in stores at these convenient times each month*:

Harlequin Presents, American Romance, Historical, Intrigue:

> May titles: April 10
> June titles: May 8
> July titles: June 5
> August titles: July 10

Harlequin Romance, Superromance, Temptation, Regency Romance:

> May titles: April 24
> June titles: May 22
> July titles: June 19
> August titles: July 24

We hope this new schedule is convenient for you.

With only two trips each month to your local bookseller, you'll never miss any of your favorite authors!

*Please note: There may be slight variations in on-sale dates in your area due to differences in shipping and handling.

*Applicable to U.S. only.

HDATES-RR